Night picked the lock and snuck into the room where Holly was being held captive…

She lay on a dirty cot, sobbing. At the sight of her anguish, the anger he'd felt at her for denying him knowledge of his son dissipated. He went to her, his steps so silent that she didn't hear him until he slid down beside her. She cried out and rolled over to fight him.

"Shh, look at me, Holly. Quiet now."

Her green eyes widened. Then recognition dawned and she nodded. The sadness in her expression was so strong that Night couldn't help himself—he pulled her into his arms and cradled her against him.

"Are you all right? Did they hurt you?" His words were a mere whisper in the cave of a room.

"I'm okay. I saw our baby."

Dear Harlequin Intrigue Reader,

The holidays are upon us! We have six dazzling stories of intrigue that will make terrific stocking stuffers—not to mention a well-deserved reward for getting all your shopping done early....

Take a breather from the party planning and unwrap Rita Herron's latest offering, *A Warrior's Mission*—the next exciting installment of COLORADO CONFIDENTIAL, featuring a hot-blooded Cheyenne secret agent! Also this month, watch for *The Third Twin*—the conclusion of Dani Sinclair's HEARTSKEEP trilogy that features an identical triplet heiress marked for murder who seeks refuge in the arms of a rugged lawman.

The joyride continues with *Under Surveillance* by highly acclaimed author Gayle Wilson. This second book in the PHOENIX BROTHERHOOD series has an undercover agent discovering that his simple surveillance job of a beautiful woman-in-jeopardy is filled with complications. Be there from the start when B.J. Daniels launches her brand-new miniseries, CASCADES CONCEALED, about a close-knit northwest community that's visited by evil. Don't miss the first unforgettable title, *Mountain Sheriff.*

As a special gift-wrapped treat, three terrific stories in one volume. Look for *Boys in Blue* by reader favorites Rebecca York, Ann Voss Peterson and Patricia Rosemoor about three long-lost New Orleans cop brothers who unite to reel in a killer. And rounding off a month of nonstop thrills and chills, a pregnant woman and her wrongly incarcerated husband must set aside their stormy past to bring the real culprit to justice in *For the Sake of Their Baby* by Alice Sharpe.

Best wishes to all of our loyal readers for a joyous holiday season!

Enjoy,

Denise O'Sullivan
Senior Editor
Harlequin Intrigue

A WARRIOR'S MISSION

RITA HERRON

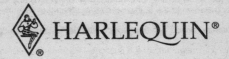

HARLEQUIN®

TORONTO • NEW YORK • LONDON
AMSTERDAM • PARIS • SYDNEY • HAMBURG
STOCKHOLM • ATHENS • TOKYO • MILAN • MADRID
PRAGUE • WARSAW • BUDAPEST • AUCKLAND

Special thanks and acknowledgment are given
to Rita Herron for her contribution
to the COLORADO CONFIDENTIAL series.

ISBN 0-373-22741-8

A WARRIOR'S MISSION

ABOUT THE AUTHOR

Award-winning author Rita Herron wrote her first book when she was twelve, but didn't think real people grew up to be writers. Now she writes so she doesn't have to get a *real* job. A former kindergarten teacher and workshop leader, she traded her story-telling for kids for romance, and writes romantic comedies and romantic suspense. She lives in Georgia with her own romance hero and three kids. She loves to hear from readers, so please write her at P.O. Box 921225, Norcross, GA 30092-1225, or visit her Web site at www.ritaherron.com.

Books by Rita Herron

HARLEQUIN INTRIGUE

HARLEQUIN AMERICAN ROMANCE

*The Hartwell Hope Chests
†Nighthawk Island

The Confidential Code

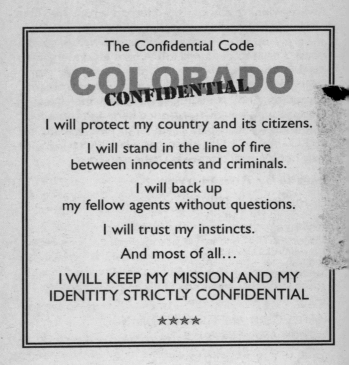

COLORADO
CONFIDENTIAL

I will protect my country and its citizens.

I will stand in the line of fire
between innocents and criminals.

I will back up
my fellow agents without questions.

I will trust my instincts.

And most of all…

I WILL KEEP MY MISSION AND MY IDENTITY STRICTLY CONFIDENTIAL

★★★★

CAST OF CHARACTERS

Holly Langworthy—A mother who will do anything to rescue her kidnapped baby. Will she lose her life and her heart in the process?

Night Walker—This half-breed Colorado Confidential agent is a loner and the father of Holly's baby. His mission is to save Holly and her son, but once he rescues them, will they welcome him back into their lives?

Schyler Langworthy—An innocent baby caught in the trap of a mad scientist. Will he survive in spite of the research drug he received via his birth mother?

Samuel Langworthy—The former governor of Colorado was against Night's involvement with Holly, and has been acting suspiciously. Could he possibly have orchestrated his grandson's kidnapping to help son Joshua's campaign to keep Holly and Night apart?

Celia Langworthy—Does she hold some clue as to who might have kidnapped Holly's baby?

Dr. Theodore Grace—Celia's former husband has been conducting germ experiments on the unsuspecting public. Has he kidnapped Holly's baby to seek revenge on Samuel for marrying Celia? And just how far will he go in his research with the baby?

Governor Forbes—He's bitter about losing the election to Joshua Langworthy, but is he bitter enough to get revenge by conspiring in a kidnapping?

Carlton Sanders—The man Holly's father wanted her to marry. He has political aspirations of his own—did he have a secret motive for romancing Holly?

To Tashya, for putting together a great bible
and giving me my start six years ago.

Prologue

''Holly Langworthy's three-month-old son has been kidnapped from his crib.'' Colleen Wellesley leveled her gaze at the group of operatives she'd assembled in the secret meeting room at the Royal Flush, the 6,000-acre cattle and horse ranch where the Colorado Confidential organization based its operation. The surveillance room had videos of the ranch access points and of the ICU offices in Denver, and computers that linked to the Department of Public Safety, the DMV and other government agencies on a limited basis.

Ten years ago, Colleen had founded a private investigation agency, Investigations, Confidential and Undercover, or ICU, which took on typical P.I. work—divorces, missing persons, blackmail and other cases. Six months ago, ICU had been recruited as the newest branch of the Confidential organization, Colorado Confidential. ICU's office in Denver had become a cover for Confidential activities. The private detective business still operated on a highly selective level, but most of the work now was done for the DPS and the federal government.

Confidential agent Night Walker jerked his head toward his boss in shock.

Holly Langworthy had a child?

The beautiful, chestnut-haired, sexy and pampered daughter of Samuel Langworthy, the former governor? Holly—the woman he had shared one incredible night with before her father had run him off and ordered him never to darken the doors of the Langworthy estate again?

"Everyone, this is my brother, Michael." Colleen continued. "I've asked him to join us today to offer suggestions and observations."

Night tuned out the introductions. His mind was still reeling from the bombshell Colleen had just dropped about Holly Langworthy. Did Colleen know about his previous relationship with Holly?

How old was the baby?

Fiona Clark and Shawn Jameson, two other Confidential agents, sat across from him, their expressions unreadable.

"Although the Langworthy family had not made public the fact that they have a grandchild," Colleen said, "the baby has been living with his mother at the Langworthy estate in Denver since his birth three months ago. Holly's father, former governor, Samuel Langworthy, has suggested that the kidnapping is connected to the upcoming gubernatorial election." Colleen continued, "Of course, now that the media has gotten wind of the story, it will be major news."

Really major news, since the former governor

was a millionaire and his son Joshua was firmly entrenched in the upcoming election as a prime candidate. Even more major news as Night mentally counted back the months and realized the baby might very well be his own son.

A son Holly Langworthy had not bothered to tell him existed.

NIGHT STRUGGLED with the idea that he might have a son as he drove at record-breaking speed away from the Royal Flush, located between Fairplay and Garo, toward the Langworthy mansion in Denver. All his life he had been a loner. His father had died when Night was little, leaving his white mother to raise him in a world that hadn't wanted her Cheyenne half-breed son. She'd eventually taken him to live on one of the reservations, hoping the people there would be more welcoming, but he had felt just as alone in the midst of his native American Indian cousins as he had in his mother's world.

He had never expected to have a family. Had blamed his father for leaving him, had thought that loving meant only pain. Especially when love involved the mixture of cultures.

But that one night with Holly had lingered in his mind. He had wanted to see her again, to call her, to touch her, yet he'd known a relationship between them would never work. Had she given birth to his son? A son who might need him?

A son who had crossed the lines between the Cheyenne and the white man, just as he had?

The snowcapped peaks of the Colorado mountains became a hazy blur as the facts of the case imprinted themselves in his brain. According to Colleen, Holly was distraught and had been avoiding the press since the kidnapping. The Langworthys had suggested that Governor Todd Houghton and his buddy Senator Franklin Gettys had instigated the kidnapping to distract Joshua Langworthy from his campaign. In turn, Governor Houghton suggested the Langworthys had staged the kidnapping to garner sympathy for Joshua in the election. Either scenario sounded feasible.

Both disgusted Night.

The odd details of the crime had the police perplexed. How had a kidnapper breached the walls of the Langworthy mansion? Langworthy had topnotch security. Night should know—he'd worked security detail at the estate a year ago. Was there someone on the inside who'd been a conspirator?

The other details were odd, too. Traces of Merino sheep wool, eggshells and dirt from the southern part of Colorado had been found at the scene, in baby Langworthy's nursery. Colleen had sent Fiona to check out Governor Houghton and Senator Gettys's ex-wife, Helen Gettys. Michael was assigned to check out the Merino sheep ranch partially owned by Gettys. Shawn was staying on with Colleen.

She had assigned Night to watch Holly.

He had a helluva lot more than watching in mind. Holly owed him some answers. And if she'd had anything to do with staging her own baby's disappearance, if that child was Night's...

The fury and anguish he felt at the realization that he might have a son he had known nothing about obliterated his ill-spent desire for Holly. Protective instincts unlike anything he'd ever felt before rose to the surface for the infant. The thought of any child, much less his own offspring, missing, being in danger, being used as a pawn in some kind of political game sickened him. The other possibilities that lurked behind the obvious political ones were even more maddening.

But what if the baby wasn't his? Would he be able to tell by looking into Holly's eyes?

He barely noticed the Denver lights as he maneuvered through traffic toward the Capitol Hill area, his mind on autopilot as he made his way to the Langworthy estate. He gave his name at the security gate to the fenced-in Victorian mansion, wondering if Langworthy had blackballed his name from the acceptance list, but as Colleen had promised, he got through with no problem. Apparently, the ex-governor wanted ICU's help badly enough to tolerate him. Emotions breathed like a fireball in his belly as he drove down the long drive to the house.

His hand trembled as he lifted the photograph Colleen had given him of Holly's son. The Langworthys had released the picture to the public in an attempt to find out who had taken the three-month-old infant from their home in the middle of the night.

In the picture, the chubby little boy was wrapped in a blue blanket, lying in his crib, a cuddly brown teddy bear snuggled beside him. Night studied the infant's features. The baby had black hair but he couldn't quite tell the color of his eyes.

Did he have his brown eyes or Holly's laughing green eyes?

Thinking of Holly sent an ache through his chest. Photographs of her and the man she'd been dating had been plastered all over the news the past few months. Carlton Sanders—a man who worked for Joshua Langworthy, a cultured man Samuel would approve of, a man suited to Holly's status. Could Carlton Sanders be the father of Holly's baby? Or was Night the father?

He touched the name bead necklace circling his neck, the one symbol of his heritage he carried with him at all times. Pride filled him at the memory of his mother's gift. If Holly and he had a child, he wanted to pass that name on to his son, give him beads to symbolize the Walker name.

A dozen lights twinkled around the stately Victorian mansion as he dragged his gaze to the doorway then upward to the window of Holly's room. Memories bombarded him. The first night he'd come to work security at the mansion. His admiration for Samuel Langworthy and all that the Centennial family had done for Colorado. His instant attraction to Langworthy's beautiful daughter, Holly.

An attraction he'd known could go nowhere.

She was rich and spoiled, and he'd pegged her flirtations as those of a rebellious princess wanting to defy daddy by taking a walk on the wild side with the hired help—a half breed at that. But her feminine wiles had been nearly irresistible. She had reminded him of the wild horses he had tamed in the past, eliciting forbidden fantasies of taming her as well. Still, he had resisted at first, walked away from her a dozen times. But in a weak moment, he had told her about the legend of Lillian's Leap. In the romantic story, his ancestors, North and Lily, escaped from danger by jumping off a cliff then landing on a hidden ledge and diving into the river below. Holly's passion and youthful romanticisms had gotten to him, had been a balm to his jaded soul.

Then she had touched him. Had lifted a slender hand to trail down the side of his face, then lower to his chest, and lower still. And finally, she'd looked into his eyes, begging him to take her. Even then he'd restrained himself, but finally her lips had brushed his, torturing him, hungry and searching. He had lost control and made love to her.

The passion had been hotter than any he'd ever experienced. Holly's body was a sultry haven in the midst of a world of corruption, her innocence so sweet it was erotic, primal. He'd wanted to taste it forever.

Yet, he'd had to leave. Especially when Holly's father had discovered them together. That humiliating encounter was etched into his brain with painful clarity. Night was the hired help, a half breed who was fit to protect the former governor's precious daughter, but not to touch her.

Samuel had thrown him out, his threats to ruin Night if he dirtied the doors of the estate again a staunch reminder of the man's power and position, and Night's lack thereof. Night had dealt with people like that before. The incident with Charity Carmichael for one. Her accusations had dogged him and always would.

This time, Night had known Langworthy was

right—he and Holly were not meant to be together. She was lightness to his dark, a society heiress who belonged to the prominent Centennial family, while he was an ex-bounty hunter who belonged to himself and his job. So he had left. And, barring the dreams that haunted his nights, dreams of lying with her again, slick hot skin against her writhing form, he had never looked back.

Until now.

A wry chuckle rumbled from deep within his chest, filled with pain, as he opened the car door and inhaled the scent of freshly manicured lawn and money. Of course, even now, he'd returned to the Langworthy mansion as a special agent to investigate a crime, not as Holly's lover.

Or as her baby's father.

HOLLY HEARD the explosion in the foyer all the way up the winding staircase to her bedroom. The housekeeper's low voice, a man's angry one demanding to see her, her father's commanding tone ordering the man to leave. Her mother's soft cry for her father to listen.

"I'm here on official business, looking into the kidnapping of your grandson, Mr. Langworthy," the man said in a tone so cold that a shiver chased up Holly's spine. "And I'm not leaving until I speak with your daughter."

"I was expecting another ICU agent, not you," her father said.

"All our agents are working the case in one capacity or another. Colleen sent me here."

Holly's heart pounded as she realized the source of the familiar voice.

Night Walker had finally returned.

She had been expecting him any day, had known this moment would arrive, that she would have to face him. She had dreaded it with all her being.

He would never understand. Never forgive her.

One trembling hand went to her now flat stomach. The other clutched baby Sky's stuffed bunny, Bun-Bun, to her chest, the scent of the baby powder and her son's soft skin that lingered on it bringing a fresh wave of tears to her eyes. She had cried so much already....

But it hadn't brought her son back. And neither had her father or the police.

Maybe Night would be able to do something.

She reached for the doorknob, ready to face his wrath when the door suddenly opened and Night appeared, her father on his heels, her mother's fine-boned hand pulling at her father's sleeve.

Most people thought Celia Langworthy a delicate flower of a woman who did as Holly's father dictated, but Holly knew differently. Celia was smart and fiercely loving. She would also do anything for Samuel and her children. And her grandson.

"Please, Samuel, we have to do whatever we can to find the baby," Celia pleaded.

Her father tried to get around Night to block the doorway, but Night overpowered him, his six-four, two-hundred pound body a menacing presence beside her petite mother. Holly drank in Night's features as he charged into the room. She remembered the way he had looked that evening so long ago when he'd held her naked in his arms. The night he had taken her virginity and they had made a son.

His classically high cheekbones and dark coloring testified to his Cheyenne heritage. His pitch-black hair still brushed his collar and made her ache to run her hands through it. But his golden brown eyes raked over her without a trace of the desire they had that night. Instead, they pinned her to the spot with accusations.

The first time she'd seen Night Walker, she had been infatuated with the mysterious, enigmatic Native American. He was soulful, intense, a creature of the shadows. A loner who had found his place in the world, a solitary place he allowed no one to enter.

What a fool she'd been, certain that their passion was all that mattered. That she could breach those forbidden walls and touch the man within.

But she had grown up fast when he'd disappeared from her life. Even more quickly with her subsequent pregnancy.

"I'm here about the kidnapping," he said without preamble. "ICU sent me."

Samuel cleared his throat. "I don't want you working on this case."

"That's not up to you, sir." Night faced her father, the two men going eye for eye as if wild animals ready for battle.

Holly clutched her arms around her stomach, her insides quivering. Her father had been acting strangely ever since Sky had been kidnapped. She was sure he was keeping things from her. Maybe to protect her. Maybe not. Whichever, she didn't give a flip about who he wanted on the case. She was tired of being out of the loop, protected, depending on others.

She wanted her baby found.

"Daddy, let me talk to him."

"Yes," Celia said, dragging her husband out the door. "Maybe he can help."

"Then let's go to my office," her father said.

"No. I want to speak to Holly in private," Night demanded.

Holly's father shook his head. "Absolutely not."

Emotions clouded Holly's eyes. "Please, Daddy. I'll be all right."

Her father exchanged a charged look with Night, then relented, his body rigid. Night waited until her parents' footsteps receded before he stalked toward her. Anger rolled off him in waves.

She stepped backward, her legs nearly buckling. Had he guessed the baby was his? "Night..."

"Show me the nursery."

His sharp order took her off guard. She'd been certain he was going to ask her. Maybe he expected her to speak up....

His hand seized her arm and she winced, then he propelled her through the door and dragged her down the hall.

"Is it this way? Downstairs by the servants' quarters so the nanny could hear him?"

His insult rankled. He assumed she was so spoiled she'd turn her baby over to a nanny? "No, it's right here, beside my room." She halted and jerked her arm free from his grip. "The adjoining bathroom made it easy to slip through and feed him during the night. I didn't want him to wake up alone.''

His eyes softened just a fraction, but his tight mouth didn't falter. Again, she thought he might ask about Sky's parentage, but he didn't. Maybe her father was right, maybe he didn't want to know.

"He's been missing a week?''

"Yes.'' She ached just thinking of the empty days and nights since she'd last held him. The hours she'd spent pacing and worrying, wondering who had stolen her son and what horrible things might have happened to him.

What had she done with her time before she'd had a baby? She couldn't bear to think about going on now, doing mindless paperwork for her father's investments.

"But you didn't hear anyone come into the nursery and take him?''

Guilt assailed her as she shook her head. She should have heard something. She should have known he was in trouble. She should have been able to save her son.

"How did someone get past the security on the mansion?''

"I...don't know.''

He gave her a suspicious look, as if he'd heard the rumors about the Langworthys staging the kidnapping to get sympathy for Joshua and believed them. Then he stepped inside the room, hesitating a second as his gaze scanned the simple decor. The native American border with mountains and bear and buffalo circling the room, the adobe color accented with navy and dark red and greens. Colors that had reminded her of Night and his heritage.

He stalked toward the crib, his trained gaze seemingly scrutinizing every feature.

"Tell me what happened the night he was kidnapped."

Oh, God, did she have to relive it all again? "I've already told the police."

"I read the report. I want to hear it from you."

She swallowed, clasping her hands together, trying to block out the worst of the memory as she recited the details. If it helped, she'd tell her story a thousand times. Everything except the evening with Carlton Sanders. "I...I had been out."

"With Sanders?" His gaze shot to hers with more accusations. Then she realized what he thought, that Carlton was her baby's father.

She refused to talk about Carlton with Night. *Especially* with Night. "When I got home, I checked on the baby. He stirred, and I gave him a bottle."

He simply stared at her, so she cleared her throat and continued. "I put him back down, tucked the covers around him, then went to bed." There was more, but she couldn't admit it. Not and watch his face twist with more disdain. He'd already decided she'd jumped straight from his bed to another man's, when, God help her, the truth was she had never been with or wanted any man except Night.

"And you never heard a sound? No footsteps, door opening, the baby didn't cry?"

She shook her head. "I was exhausted, I hadn't been sleeping much, I don't know how...why he didn't cry." Her voice broke off and she looked away, unable to keep the emotions at bay or tell him about the sedative she'd taken. The one she had refused, but the one she suspected their maid, Antonia, had slipped into her tea to calm her from the ordeal with her father and the man he'd wanted her to marry.

Night studied her for a long moment as if he was trying to strip her defenses and read her mind, uncover her secrets. Then he slowly dropped his gaze back to the crib. He ran his strong hands over the edge of the baby bed, stroking the blanket as if it held a connection to him or might offer him answers as to who had taken Schyler. His jaw was a solid rock, his cheekbones so defined her heart squeezed. Her son would share that same profile one day.

"The baby's name is Schyler?" His voice sounded more hoarse than normal, strains of his Native heritage filtering through.

She nodded, her heart breaking. "North Schyler Langworthy."

A muscle twitched in his jaw. The flare of anguish that deepened his brown eyes to black sucked the air from her lungs.

Now, he knew the baby was his.

He remembered telling her that romantic story about his ancestors.

How could he even think she'd been with another man after that incredible evening?

"I'm sorry, Night...I—" her voice broke, the pain of the last week, of her father's humiliating accusations the evening Night had walked out of her life resurfacing. Her father had never let her forget the depth of her sins for taking Night to her bed.

Especially when he had discovered she was pregnant. And Night had never looked back. She had needed him....

"Did you ever plan to tell me I had a son?"

"I...wanted to," Holly said, knowing her excuse would sound weak to his ears. But she had to try to make him understand. "You left and you never called, you never came back. I didn't know how to contact you."

"You didn't try." Steely rage underscored his softly spoken words.

She shook her head violently. In spite of her father's fury, she had tried to find Night. "I did look for you, but you just disappeared, and then I...I was ashamed that I'd seduced you. You'd told me all along that you didn't want me, that you would never be tied down, that you were like a wild wolf, free forever." Her words rushed out, the contempt in his expression seemingly mounting with every word she spoke. "I didn't think you'd want to be trapped into marrying me. And I was afraid you'd think I got pregnant on purpose."

He squared his shoulders, fisting his hands by his sides as if fighting for control. "You were going to marry Sanders and let him raise my baby as his? Were you seeing him before the night we were together?"

"No." Holly felt the color drain from her face. He couldn't know the truth.

"Did Sanders kidnap the baby? Is he working for your father?"

"What?"

"Did your family arrange this kidnapping to get

publicity for Joshua's campaign?'' He pinned her with a look that burned straight through to her soul. ''Did you help them or did Sanders? Are you hiding our baby somewhere until after your brother is elected governor?''

She staggered backward at the depth of his distrust. ''No,'' she whispered. ''Heavens, no. I swear it.'' Defenses she hadn't known she possessed flourished, then anger followed. ''How can you suggest such a horrible thing? You have no idea the hell I've been through. You walked out of here the night we were together and left me alone to deal with everything, my father, the pregnancy. You never once looked back or tried to contact me. What was I supposed to think?''

''I had no idea you were pregnant because you didn't bother to tell me,'' he ground out. ''Your family kept it a secret until the baby was kidnapped.''

''They were trying to avoid a media frenzy,'' Holly argued. ''And Daddy wanted to protect me. It's not like you actually cared. I didn't think you wanted me, much less a baby.''

''I do want my son,'' he said, his words cold and clipped, leaving no doubt in her mind that he didn't want her. ''And make no mistake, Holly, when I find our baby, he will know his father. And his heritage.''

He gave her one last look of disgust, then turned and stalked down the stairs, his booted feet clacking on the marble foyer just before the door slammed behind him.

Holly leaned over the crib, tears overflowing.

Another reason she hadn't contacted him—her father had warned her that Night might try to take the baby from her, that the laws might even give him custody, let him carry their son to live on one of the reservations. She'd even wondered if Night might have discovered she'd had his baby and kidnapped him himself. And when her worst fears had overwhelmed her this past week, when she'd pictured her helpless infant at the mercy of a crazy person or a killer, she'd actually hoped that Night might have taken him. At least then she would know her son was safe.

But Night obviously hadn't.

Her world spun, crumbling around her.

Where was her precious little boy? Was he still alive? She looked up through the window at the inky sky.

Was he out there somewhere, alone and scared, crying for his mother?

Chapter One

Late November

Where was her baby?

It had been four months since he'd gone missing. She'd thought for sure she'd have him back in her arms by Thanksgiving. Now Thanksgiving had come and gone.

Holly sat on the edge of her seat in her father's study, twisting her sweating hands together, as she waited on him to finish the phone call.

Something was wrong.

She saw it in the way her father pulled at his chin and angled his face away from her. Between his hushed phone calls with the FBI and local police the past few days, the barrage of extra security on the house, the press hounding them and the claustrophobic feel of hiding out between the walls of the mansion for the past four months, her nerves had reached the hysteria level.

Why hadn't they received a ransom note?

Why hadn't someone called with information?

And why didn't her father tell her everything that was going on?

With every day that passed, the chances of finding her son grew slimmer and slimmer. She wasn't sure she could take it anymore.

Her father dropped the phone into its cradle, sighed and pivoted in his leather chair to face her. His expression looked worried, but commanding, as always. Once again, she sensed he was holding back, hiding things from her. Why?

"Did they find anything?"

Her father shook his head slowly, drumming fingers on his chin. "I'm sorry, sweetheart. There's no news."

"There's something," Holly said, her voice a mere whisper. "I can see it in your eyes, Daddy. Now, tell me."

He hesitated, then looked back at Holly's mother, who had moved to stand behind him, one delicate hand placed on his shoulder. Her mother—the weaker one on the surface, but behind the scenes, the rock of the family, the one always offering support.

"I'm afraid the FBI's ready to call this a cold case. They'll leave the phone surveillance intact, but may have to pull back some on the investigation. Other cases…"

He let the sentence trail off and Holly sucked in a sharp breath. "They can't give up."

"I didn't say they were giving up," her father said. "Just pulling back. And ICU is still on the case."

Holly glared at her dad. "What are you keeping

from me? They found him, didn't they? They found him and he's dead, but you're afraid to tell me.''

''No, Holly, good Lord. Calm down.'' Her father raked a hand over his face. ''There's really no other news. I wish there was.''

She pressed a hand to her mouth to calm her emotions. She couldn't stand the waiting. And her father knew more than he was confiding in her. She was certain of it.

The tension between them had been almost unbearable, since her confrontation with Night. During her pregnancy, Holly had suspected that her father had had some part in keeping Night away from her. Lately she had even wondered if he had orchestrated Schyler's disappearance to punish her or teach her a lesson for seducing Night, or to gain sympathy for Joshua's campaign. Politics meant everything to her father. But now Joshua had won the election. If that had been the motive for the kidnapping, there was no longer a reason to keep Sky from home.

Sometimes, her dad seemed genuinely concerned, as if he was really worried about her and his grandchild. As if he feared some horrible thing had happened to her baby. But he had been keeping the details of the case from her, treating her like a child, and she couldn't stand it any longer.

''You know, sweetheart,'' he said in a low tone, ''you…we all might have to come to terms with the fact that we might never find Schyler.''

''What?'' Holly gasped. She must have heard him wrong.

Celia pressed a shaky hand to her mouth, then moved toward Holly, reaching out her arms. ''I

don't want to hear that either,'' she said. ''But your
father's right. This ordeal is killing you, I can see
it—''

Tears burned Holly's eyes. ''You don't care if we
get my baby back!''

''That's not true and you know it, Holly,'' Celia
said in a more forceful voice. ''But it's tearing us
all apart, the three of us are on pins and needles. I
can't handle watching you suffer so. I see you wake
up every day with hope, then go to bed with it shattered at night. You're not eating, not sleeping.''

Holly's throat constricted. ''How can I sleep and
eat when my son is missing?''

Her father stood, shook his head and stared out
the window at the gardens beyond. ''We've done
everything we can do.''

''No!'' Her heart broke at his words. ''I will
never accept that my baby's not coming back.
Never.''

Holly backed toward the door, then spun around
and ran from the room, tears blinding her as she
took the steps two at a time to the empty nursery.

HER BABY NEEDED HER..

*Holly rolled over and squinted through the dark-
ened interior of her bedroom, the sound of her son's
cry warming her. He was safe and sound in his crib,
but he needed feeding. Again. She hadn't realized
how often infants ate, how exhausting it would be
to care for a baby.*

*How precious every moment she had with him
was until she'd lost him.*

She appreciated it now—now he'd been found and brought back to her.

Regardless of the fact that she'd just fallen asleep, Holly tossed the duvet aside, shoved her feet into her bedroom shoes and grabbed her robe. She cinched it at her waist, shoving a tangle of unruly hair from her face as she hurried through the adjoining bathroom to her son's room. The pale glow of the night-light bathed the room, her son's whimpers a soft blip in the otherwise quiet nursery.

She could already see his chubby arms waving, his legs cycling the air, kicking off the covers, his dark brown eyes scrunched, searching through the darkness for her. She began to sing his favorite lullaby in a low voice to let him know she was there, and crossed the room, anxious to hold him to her breast, the tingle of anticipation already seeping through her, making her feel giddy.

She had never known she could love a baby so much. Had never known she could feel so much pain when he had been ripped from her life.

He lay curled on his side, covered in the crocheted blanket her mother had given him when Holly had brought him home. She gently eased it aside. "Come on, sweetheart. Mommy's here. We're never going to be separated again."

A scream lodged in her throat.

Her baby was gone! Nooooo. Not again.

Tears swam to her eyes as she frantically searched every corner of the crib. But her efforts were useless. Her baby hadn't come back. They hadn't found him at all.

He might be lost to her forever....

HOLLY'S EYES flew open, a sob wrenching from deep inside her as she leaned over Sky's empty crib. How many times in the past four months had she been entrenched in this nightmare and walked in her sleep to her son's room? Tears flowed down her cheeks and dripped onto her hands as she dropped her head onto the railing and cried.

Why hadn't they found him? Who had stolen her baby from his crib? Why would someone torture her like this? Maybe she had been spoiled, a rich girl, had played with fire by seducing Night, but she loved Sky, and he…he didn't deserve this.

Her chest heaved with her sobs, the hope she'd clung to the first week he'd been kidnapped dwindling every day. And now the FBI and her father were practically giving up. Even the P.I.s working on the case hadn't caught the kidnapper.

A shrill sound cut through her misery and she jerked her head toward her bedroom. The phone was ringing. Not a house phone though, her cell phone. Who would be calling this time of night?

Someone about the search? Night maybe? She'd barely talked to him since he'd stormed out. But she knew he had been watching her.

Knew he blamed her, as she blamed herself.

The price she had paid for her passion…would her misery ever end?

The sharp ring drowned out her thoughts, and she dashed through the bathroom and flipped on a light, scanning the clumps of clothes and accessories littering the dresser and her chaise lounge for the phone. Where was her purse?

Panicked now, she tossed items haphazardly onto

the floor, digging beneath the rubble until her hands landed on the oversize leather bag she'd purchased to double as a small diaper bag. She'd wanted to be a fashionable young mother.

Now, she would trade every cent the Langworthys had to hold her baby again.

The phone trilled again and she turned the bag upside down and dumped the contents. Lipstick, brush, wallet, powder—cell phone. Sighing with relief, she punched the button and held it to her ear. "Hello."

"Holly Langworthy?"

"Yes." She frowned, the hair at the nape of her neck rising. She didn't recognize the gruff voice.

"If you want to see your son again, listen carefully."

Her heart hammered against her ribs. This was the phone call they'd been waiting for. Her legs gave way and she collapsed onto the plush carpet, unable to believe it—she might get Sky back. "Wh—what do you want me to do?"

"Meet me at the Langworthy cabin at dawn."

Her hands trembled as she fought her emotions. "Is my son all right?"

"Just show up. And, Holly…" His breath wheezed out. "Come alone. If I see a cop, or even a hint of one, you'll never see your baby again."

REGARDLESS OF the late hour, Colleen Wellesley had called a meeting at the Royal Flush to discuss the Langworthy baby kidnapping. Most of the key Confidential agents were there—Shawn Jameson,

Ryan Benton, Colleen's brother Michael, Fiona Clark, Conrad Burke, and Night.

The Confidential operatives had been working round the clock for the past four months. Although the FBI was pulling back, Samuel Langworthy still wanted Colorado Confidential, known to him as ICU, on the case. Thank God.

But even if Langworthy or Colorado Confidential gave up, Night wouldn't.

His co-workers had no idea how powerless he felt without answers. Or how Night wanted them to use the Walker name instead of Langworthy when they referred to his son. Not that Samuel Langworthy would ever allow that to happen....

"Okay," Colleen said after calling the meeting to order. "Let's recap what we've learned so far." She gestured toward her brother Michael. "Traces of wool, dirt, and egg shells were found by the baby's crib. The wool fibers were from Merino sheep. I sent Michael undercover to the Half Spur, a Merino sheep ranch partially owned by Senator Gettys, to see if there might be evidence to connect him to the kidnapping."

Michael took the floor first. "The atmosphere at the Half Spur was secretive and strange. Blood was collected from the flock at regular intervals. We lifted one of the blood samples and sent it to the Fort Collins CDC for testing. The sheep's blood tested positive for a strange virus and antibodies for a bacteria called *Coxiella burnetii,* which causes Q fever. It seems the sheep are a test flock for a self-spreading vaccine for Q fever." Michael paused.

"I received an e-mail from Wiley Longbottom,

the director of the DPS,'' Colleen added. ''He saw those CDC results and suggested we check out a flu that hit Silver Rapids early this year.'' She indicated for Shawn to continue.

''About five months prior to the kidnapping, a flu hit Silver Rapids. The people were treated at Gilpin Hospital in Denver. Two died.'' Shawn pressed his hands on the table. ''At about the same time the kidnapping occurred, Gilpin's records room was damaged in a fire.''

''Too much of a coincidence,'' Night said.

''Exactly. We caught the arsonist but he claims to know nothing about the kidnapping,'' Shawn explained. ''But we're sure that the experiments being done on the sheep ranch are connected to the Silver Rapids flu. Dr. Kelley Stanton—'' Shawn flushed as he said the name of the woman Night knew had captured his heart ''—discovered that the flu was actually a Q fever outbreak. The people of Silver Rapids were probably exposed to a live version of whatever was being tested on the Half Spur flock.

''Senator Gettys still insists that Samuel Langworthy staged the kidnapping for publicity for his son Joshua. Former governor Todd Houghton seems to be in agreement.''

With Holly's knowledge or without? Night had watched her from a distance these past four months, had seen the strain on her face, the dark circles beneath her eyes that showed she wasn't sleeping. Even though she loved her brother Joshua and Night still resented the fact that she had kept his son from him, he didn't believe she'd be a party to such a plan.

Ryan Benton jumped in. "While Michael was at the Half Spur, I investigated Helen Gettys, the senator's former wife."

Night turned his attention to Ryan, who explained that the senator was under investigation by the FBI for experimenting with biological weapons. Helen Gettys had given Ryan computer disks, copied from the Half Spur, that all but proved Gettys was involved in experiments that were likely illegal.

"When Senator Gettys was questioned about the experiments being done on the ranch, he was sweating," Ryan stated. "He definitely supports bio research and wants to make Colorado the location of a premier research facility once the 1972 bio weapons treaty limitations are reassessed. But he insists there is no connection between the germs tested on his sheep and the Silver Rapids flu."

"What about Joshua Langworthy?" Night asked.

"He's clear," Fiona said with a sly grin. While investigating Joshua, Fiona had developed a personal relationship with Holly's half brother, the governor elect. Now she and Joshua were engaged.

"And Houghton probably isn't too happy about losing the election," Night noted.

Fiona shrugged. "He's a little bitter toward Joshua and Samuel Langworthy. Joshua admits that his father has been acting strangely and thinks we should keep an eye on him."

Night frowned. Back to Holly's father. Would he kidnap his own grandson to gain publicity for Joshua's campaign? Or perhaps he had orchestrated the kidnapping to punish Holly for getting involved with Night? What if Langworthy had decided he didn't want a half-breed baby tainting the image of the Centennial family and decided to get him out of the picture completely? That would explain the reason there had been no ransom—and how someone had breached Langworthy security.

"Helen Gettys confirmed a connection between Senator Gettys and mobster Helio DeMarco, now deceased," Colleen continued. "As you know, DeMarco's web of illegal activities reached worldwide. A suspicious relationship for a senator. The FBI believes that one of Helio's corporations may be the other owner of the Half Spur."

Conrad stood, scrubbing a hand over the back of his neck. "We also discovered that DeMarco's nephew Tony used Holly's half sister, Marilyn, to steal germ stock from Mills & Grommett, the pharmaceutical company affiliated with the Langworthys. Before he died, Helio implied that Holly might have inadvertently been a subject of germ testing herself."

Night nearly bolted up from the table. "What?"

Con's expression turned grave. "Tony tricked Marilyn into bringing Holly to Silver Rapids during her pregnancy. We think Holly was exposed to the germ test that caused the Silver Rapids flu."

Night inhaled to control his emotions, although his pulse raced as he realized the implications. Both for Holly and their son. How many people had died of the Silver Rapids flu? "Has she been ill?"

"Holly suffered from symptoms during the Silver Rapids epidemic, in her seventh month of pregnancy, and was sick for four days," Con answered. "Her symptoms also matched Q fever."

"What are the long-term effects?" Night asked.

"None that we know of, but she'll definitely need follow-up tests."

Night nodded.

"And the baby?" *His* son?

"We have no way of knowing." Colleen gave him a sympathetic look.

"Why subject a pregnant woman to germ testing?" Night asked. "And risk the life of an unborn child?"

Con released a troubled sigh. "I may have the answer there." He met Night's concerned look with one of equal measure. "As a young child, I used to stay with Holly's mother, my Aunt Celia, when my family was out of town."

"What does that have to do with Holly?"

"Celia was married to a doctor then, Theodore Grace. Dr. Grace earned his Ph.D. in microbiology at Yale where he met Celia and Samuel Langworthy. At one time, Grace was recruited to work at the federal government's biological weapons research center in Frederick, Maryland. He made breakthrough discoveries and was working on highly promising experiments in combining viral and bacterial DNA when President Nixon shut down bio weapons research in 1969."

A deathly chill invaded Night's body. He had heard the name before. "But he didn't give up the research?"

Con shook his head.

"No, he became obsessed, moody and abusive to my aunt. He built a home laboratory, locked himself in it for days and continued testing." He sighed.

"One weekend, when I was sick and Aunt Celia was taking care of me, Grace gave me an experimental bacterial concoction to boost my immune system. That was the last straw for Aunt Celia. When she discovered he'd used me as a guinea pig, she divorced him shortly after."

"No surprise there," Colleen said. "And later, Celia married Samuel Langworthy."

Con nodded. "Teddy Grace is one of the few people capable of producing the designer germs Helio DeMarco liked to play with. Grace is connected to the Langworthys through Celia. He's certainly capable of testing germs on an unknowing public, such as the people of Silver Rapids."

And on Holly and his son. But why them?

To get revenge on Samuel Langworthy and his wife, Celia?

"For now, all our leads go back to Grace," Colleen said. "Not only does he hate Samuel Langworthy for stealing Celia away from him, but, if he was involved in the Silver Rapids flu, he might want to follow up on the germ test to see how it affected Holly's unborn child."

Night folded his hands in front of him, his calm demeanor a mere smoke screen. Inside, his heart was raging, his anger like a bomb ready to explode.

"So our next step," Colleen said, "is to find Teddy Grace."

"I'm taking this assignment." Night stood, ready for action. "Any idea where he is?"

Colleen shook her head. "Not yet, but we're looking into it."

Night headed toward the door. "I'll go to the

Langworthys and see if Celia has heard from him. Maybe she can give us a clue where to find him.''

Hopefully, finding Grace would lead Night to his baby.

''We'll pinpoint areas where his lab might be,'' Colleen said. ''The dirt found by Baby Sky's crib may have come from Southeast Colorado.''

''I'll call you from the Langworthys and get the coordinates,'' Night said.

Colleen hesitated. ''All right. But once you find the location, wait for backup. You are not to go in to Grace's laboratory alone. We have no idea what we're up against.''

He nodded.

Good God. With all that he'd just learned, Colleen was crazy to think he'd wait for backup. If he found the lab and thought his son was inside, he would do whatever he had to do to rescue him.

SHOULD SHE tell someone where she was going?

Come alone. If I see a cop or even a hint of one, you'll never see your baby again.

The caller's words echoed in Holly's head, nearly making her legs buckle. But she couldn't be weak now. This was her chance to save her baby. To redeem herself for her son and prove to Night that she deserved to have his child.

Still, what if the call had been a setup? The man hadn't mentioned a ransom, which was odd in itself. She'd been certain the kidnapper would want money. But as time passed, when she hadn't received a ransom note, she'd wondered…

Why had the caller told her to go to the cabin? Because it was deserted?

The timing of the phone call didn't escape her either. She had heard nothing for four months and now this call, only days after the election was over and Joshua had taken office, when her father said the FBI was pulling back, when he'd tried to convince her to give up—a nagging suspicion took hold that her father and his campaign cronies might have orchestrated the kidnapping and now that Joshua was in office, had decided to return the baby. Where better to meet her than someplace deserted, someplace owned by their family, someplace where they might leave the baby or be able to convince her not to press charges?

And if her father wasn't involved and was giving up on finding Sky, if the FBI was pulling back, then *she* had to do something. Because she would never give up.

Her hands trembled as she threw off her robe. For a brief second, she considered calling Night for help.

But his bitter parting words still stung, and she had to hurry. Maybe, just maybe, her prayers had been answered and she would have her son back in her arms for Christmas.

Then maybe Night could forgive her. And she could forgive herself.

She scribbled a note and left it on her dresser, explaining she had received a phone call, maybe a lead to where Sky was, and that she had gone to check it out. She wouldn't disturb Celia—her poor mother had suffered almost as much as Holly had the past few months. No, Holly would have her cell phone with her and would call as soon as she made it to the cabin and was reunited with Sky.

Realizing winter had already descended, she dressed in warm socks, hiking boots, jeans and a T-shirt, and threw a denim shirt over the ensemble. She stuffed her cell phone back into her purse, checked to make sure she still had the mace she carried for protection, and packed a backpack full of baby supplies—diapers, formula, water, baby wipes. And she couldn't forget Bun-Bun. She kissed the bunny's nose, then stuck it in the bag. Then she retrieved the small pistol her father had bought her to take to the cabin. He'd insisted she carry some kind of protection when she traveled there alone. It had been the gun or a bodyguard. She'd chosen the .22.

Anticipation zinged through her as she grabbed her coat, gloves and hat and slipped out the back door. Late evening shadows blackened the walls, nearly obliterating her path as she found her way to her car. Traffic wouldn't be bad in the middle of the night, but she was nervous, and she didn't want to drive fast. Besides, she had several hours ahead of her. Then she'd have to get a horse and ride to the cabin.

As expected, she passed only a few cars on the highway, the mountains on both sides cresting and enfolding her in their beauty. A light snow had begun to fall, the crystals splashing her windshield like teardrops. She turned on the defroster, the haze of the storm making visibility difficult. Yet as she drew near Aspen and then turned onto the dirt road that led to the stable where the Langworthys kept horses, snow spewed behind her wheels and the sense of isolation replaced the awe of the mountains. Normally, she loved retreating to the cabin. She'd been tempted to hide out there ever since Sky had disappeared, but hadn't wanted to leave the mansion in case they received word about the baby.

Prairie land stretched before her, the onset of winter painting the landscape with a blanket of white. Darkness was giving way to predawn shades of gold and orange by the time she reached the stable. Another storm cloud hovered on the horizon, ready to rob the sun before it could explode into morning glory.

She parked by the corral and grabbed her fur-lined denim jacket, hat and gloves, hoping to leave for the cabin before any of the ranch hands discovered her mission and questioned her.

She snuck into the barn, slung the backpack onto the ground, then saddled up her favorite black and white paint, Sledge. After packing her supplies in the saddlebags, she took off toward the cabin.

The air was frigid, the wind howling through the treetops. She tugged the collar of her jacket around her neck and guided Sledge into the hills, resorting to the steep path through the woods that would shorten her journey. Riding again felt wonderfully liberating, as if the tension was ebbing away with her descent into the woods. Yet the nagging worry that the call had been a setup still dogged her.

She tamped down the worry, letting excitement spur her on—soon she would see her son again, hold him. How much had he grown? Would he even recognize her?

The fact that the caller hadn't mentioned ransom money still seemed odd. After all, her father was a millionaire. Had he orchestrated the kidnapping to gain publicity for Joshua or to teach her a lesson because she'd insisted on keeping the baby, against his wishes, and then because she'd refused to marry Carlton? Surely he wouldn't be that cruel, although he had behaved strangely the past few months. And the whole ordeal with Carlton…

She shuddered, a wolf's cry from the hills reminding her how dangerous riding alone could be. Then again, rescuing her son was worth the risk. After all, what kind of life did she have ahead if she had to go on living without her little boy?

Night's face flashed into her mind, his bitter parting words haunting her. Not only did he despise her for keeping Sky's birth a secret, but he blamed her for the kidnapping.

Her father, ashamed of her for having an illegitimate child, had kept the baby a secret because of the media, but he'd also wanted to delay public knowledge of her son in hopes he could marry her off to a respectable man—Carlton Sanders. And Night thought she was so despicable she might even have been a party in her own son's disappearance. As if the fact that he had never contacted her after the night they'd made love hadn't hurt enough.

Heavy clouds moved closer, casting an ominous feel over the forest, the spiked leaves above her creating a web of fingery shadows. She ignored the chill. In a few minutes, she might be cradling her baby in her arms. Just as she reached the clearing to the cabin, a loud roaring sound burst through the animal sounds of the forest.

A plane? No, a helicopter. Probably one of the rescue teams looking for stranded hikers or tourists. She reached the incline to the cabin, patting Sledge as rocks sprayed from beneath his hooves. "We're almost there, buddy. We're going to get Sky."

The sight of the cabin evoked bittersweet memories of happier times, but also offered hope that the torture of the past few months would soon end. She scanned the exterior for signs of life, of an intruder, even a horse or snowmobile to indicate she had company, but saw nothing. Thankfully, she'd arrived before the kidnapper. She'd have time to prepare.

Still, she approached the cabin slowly, easing up on the reins to gather her courage as well as to keep an eye on the doors and windows. Bringing the paint to a halt, she set him loose in the corral to the side of the cabin and made sure he had water. She'd wait until she checked out the cabin before she unsaddled him and put him in the barn. She might have to escape in a hurry.

Her boots crunched on the icy gravel as she walked toward the cabin. Unease clawed at her as she unlocked the door then it opened. She searched the dark interior but saw nothing. The whir of the helicopter drifted nearer, and she glanced over her shoulder just as it circled the clearing. She paused to see if it was going to land, but a shadow moved in the corner of the room. Heart pounding, she reached inside her purse for the pistol, but someone grabbed her from behind and shoved a rag over her mouth and nose. She bucked backward, struggling to breathe, digging her hands into the man's arms. She tried to scream, but tasted something strange, and inhaled a pungent odor. Some kind of chemical. Gas? Chloroform?

Desperate, she clawed at his hands, then jabbed her elbow backward to connect with the man's stomach. He grunted, then jerked her harder against him, pinning her in a viselike grip. She tried to scream again, but sucked in gas. Darkness spun into a kaleidoscope of colors. Tears rolled down her cheeks as she fell into the nothingness. She wished she could have held her baby one more time before she died.

Chapter Two

Early morning shadows hovered over the porch awning as Night rang the doorbell to the Langworthy mansion. Thankfully, Langworthy had alerted his security to allow him full access to the property. If this crazy doctor had his son, what would Grace do to him? Use him like a damn test rat? Inject him with God knows what kind of virus or bacteria?

How far would a mad scientist go in the name of research?

In light of these recent revelations, he half prayed Langworthy *had* spirited Schyler away in the guise of a kidnapping to create publicity.

The door opened and Frederickson, one of the security agents, answered. Night greeted him, then spotted the maid, Antonia, breezing in from the kitchen.

"I need to speak to Langworthy."

"Is he expecting you?"

"No." Night fisted his hands by his sides. "But I may have information about the kidnapping. I have to discuss it with him immediately."

The small Hispanic woman nodded, then gestured

for him to wait while she darted up the winding staircase. Seconds later, Langworthy stalked down the steps, looking haggard. His wife, Celia, trailed behind him belting her robe. She looked agitated and smaller than he remembered, as if the ordeal had taken its toll on her.

"Where's Holly?" the former senator bellowed.

Night froze. "What?"

"Where is she?" Langworthy scraped a hand over his jaw. "We can't find her anywhere. We thought she might have run off to meet you."

Night met Langworthy's steely gaze with a cold one of his own. "I haven't talked to her in weeks. Maybe she's off with that Sanders guy."

"No, she wouldn't…" Celia's voice broke.

"How long has she been gone?" Night asked.

"I don't know," Celia said. "She was here last night when I went to bed."

"Then she's probably just gone for a drive or something."

"No," Celia said. "She hardly leaves the house. She sits by the phone waiting on news about Schyler."

"You told Antonia you had news about the kidnapping?" Langworthy said.

Night nodded. "We have to talk."

Celia gestured toward the maid. "Antonia, please bring some coffee to Mr. Langworthy's study."

"*Si, Senora.*" The maid bustled off, and Night followed the Langworthys into the office. The expensive wood of the room closed around Night as he took a seat on the plush leather chair. Seconds later, the maid returned with a silver tray laden with coffee, and served them.

Night declined. "It's time for the truth, Langworthy. I want some answers."

"What the hell are you talking about?" Samuel Langworthy said angrily. "I'm paying your agency to give me answers."

Night still didn't trust that the politician wasn't involved in the baby's disappearance. "Tell me everything you know about Dr. Teddy Grace."

Celia gasped, and fell back against the camelback sofa. "I thought this was about Schyler?"

"It is," Night said in a grave tone. "We think Teddy Grace may have kidnapped the baby."

All the color faded from Celia's face. Samuel Langworthy swallowed hard and set his coffee down on the cherry desk. "Jesus, this can't be happening." He raised his gaze to meet Night's. "I...I actually thought you might have kidnapped my grandson, that you'd taken him to some reservation."

Night frowned. Langworthy actually sounded serious. "How could I have kidnapped my son when you kept him a secret from me? You forbade me to ever return to the Langworthy mansion."

Langworthy actually blanched. Celia was visibly shaking, her hands running up and down the coffee cup as if to warm them.

Night fought compassion for the two. He would never forgive them for hiding his son from him. If he had known about his baby, he could have protected him.

"Why do you think Teddy might be involved?" Celia asked.

"You were married to him at one time, correct?"

She nodded, despair in her eyes. "That was a long time ago."

"But he still hates me," Langworthy said, patting his wife's arm. "He blames me for stealing you from him."

"Enough to seek revenge by kidnapping your grandson?" Night asked.

Langworthy pushed a hand through his gray hair. "Hell, yes. He's a crazy SOB."

"Those last few months we were together, he became obsessed with his work, and with me," Celia said in a shaky voice. "He even became abusive."

Night dreaded telling them the rest, that Grace's motives might be even more sinister. "Have you had contact with Grace recently?"

Celia shook her head on a sob.

"No." Langworthy stretched his hands in front of him, staring at his fingers. "Although when I heard there were traces of eggshells found in the baby's room, I wondered. I remembered Celia telling me years ago that Teddy used eggs to incubate bacteria."

"And you didn't bother to tell the detectives about this?" Night asked.

Langworthy closed his eyes as if to gather his composure, then opened them and shook his head. "It was too horrible to think about. And I finally wrote it off as improbable. No one's heard from the man in years."

Night explained Gettys's possible connection to

Grace, then filled them in on the strange flu epidemic that had struck Silver Rapids and the connection ICU had made to Holly.

Celia dabbed at her eyes with a napkin. "Oh, my Lord. You think Teddy infected Holly with a virus when she was pregnant?"

"Yes," Night said. "Your nephew Con told us about the test Grace conducted on him when he was little. Since Grace didn't get to follow Con growing up, he might have kidnapped Sky to study the effect the virus he'd given Holly had on him."

"This is insane." Celia dropped her head in to her hands. "And it's all my fault. That man nearly destroyed my family years ago and now…"

"Don't, Celia," Langworthy said, "I'm to blame." He glanced up at Night, his expression pained. "Years ago, I introduced Grace to Franklin Gettys in hopes that Gettys would distract Grace from Celia—"

"Mr. and Mrs. Langworthy." Antonia burst into the room, holding a piece of paper in her trembling hand, her eyes wide with fright. "I do not think this is good. It's from Miss Holly."

"What?" Langworthy snatched the note, read the message, then clutched his chest.

Celia motioned to the maid. "Get his heart medicine. Hurry." She turned to Night. "What does it say?"

Night took the note and read it aloud. Dear God, Holly had received a message from the kidnapper and had gone off alone to find their son.

He looked at the Langworthys' faces and realized

they were both thinking the same thing he was—
that Teddy Grace might have Holly, too.

And if he did, what would he do with her?

"This is all my fault," Samuel wheezed. "I
should have told her what's going on."

"What do you mean?" Night asked.

"I've been trying to protect her." He coughed,
downing his pills with water. "I never told her the
progress ICU has been making. And last night..."
he sucked in a harsh breath. "I told her the feds
were pulling back."

Night grimaced. Holly thought they were giving
up.

Celia was crying softly. "It's my fault, too, I tried
to tell her we might have to accept the fact that
Schyler was gone forever...that she needed to go
on." She sniffed, her voice quavering. "I've been
so worried about Holly. She's been so heartbroken,
she's making herself physically ill."

Samuel pulled Celia into his arms and Night swallowed hard. Holly must have thought everyone had
given up on finding her son. That she was all alone.

He crushed the note in his hands. This was his
fault, too. He should have contacted her, been there
to comfort her, reassured her that even if everyone
else gave up, that he never would.

Now it might be too late. Grace might have her
and his son.

And if he didn't hurry and find them, he might
lose them both forever.

He reached for his phone to call Colleen. First,
he'd see if they had picked up the tracking device
he'd put on Holly's car and find out where she was

headed. Then he'd see if Colorado Confidential had narrowed down a location for Grace's lab.

He only hoped that, when he found it, Holly and their baby were still alive.

HOLLY TRIED to open her eyes, but her lids were so heavy. A bitter taste filled her mouth. Nausea rolled through her, but she fought through the wave, struggling to figure out where she was and what had happened. Had she been in an accident? Was she in the hospital?

A blurred face swam in front of her eyes, but she couldn't distinguish the person's features. Then the sharp jab of a needle pricked her arm and she tensed, memories surfacing. The dream about her baby being kidnapped. Except it wasn't a dream. It was real. The phone call. Driving, then riding out to the cabin. The sound of a helicopter. The shadow.

Dizziness overcame her again and she closed her eyes. Tears trickled down her cheeks, but she was helpless to move her arms and dry them. She just wanted to find her baby, to hold little Schyler again, to soothe his cries.

Now she might die and never see him.

Unable to fight the drugs she'd been given any longer, she slowly slipped back into the darkness, letting her mind carry her back to a happy time, to a night when she'd felt young and alive and thought anything was possible. The evening she had finally found a place in Night's arms, the time she had given herself to him with wild abandon.

THE SOUNDS *of laughter and partying, glasses clinking in celebration of the Fourth of July filled the balmy spring air on the outdoor patio, the scents of wild columbine mingling with her mother's roses in the gardens surrounding them. Holly stroked the stem of her crystal champagne flute, sipping the bubbly liquid as the guests began to depart, her gaze fixed on one man.*

Night Walker.

Her protector. He'd stood in the shadows of the festivities all evening, on the periphery of the family property as if he didn't belong. His distance served as a constant reminder that he was there to do a job, not to flirt with Holly. His efficiency impressed her, the way he constantly scanned the darkness as if he had night vision that could scope out any approaching evil. And although his gaze drifted to her throughout the evening, he'd also kept a constant check with the other security guards located around the property to confirm that the Langworthys' safety was intact.

Holly wasn't concerned for her safety. And she was not afraid of the enigmatic Native, although she sensed he had tried to make her fearful from the beginning. No, she was ready to take a walk on the wild side. She had been ever since the first day he had entered the mansion and her father had informed her he would be working security for the family. One look into his dark eyes, and she had been mesmerized by his Cheyenne manners, his rugged face, and the mysterious aura surrounding him. He moved like a black panther, stalwart and silent, his brown eyes nearly black with determination to do his job and remain uninvolved. She liked that about him. Liked his quiet assurance, the way he could make her feel things without even speaking.

He didn't like her though. But he wanted her.

She'd realized that immediately. He thought she was a spoiled princess, had told her that the first time she had tried to kiss him, had reminded her the next time she'd touched him that the two of them came from different worlds. But Holly could be stubborn as well. Words didn't matter. Emotions did.

Granted she'd been pampered, suffocated actually to the point she hadn't had a chance to live, to test the waters with a man. Now, she was hungry for the kind of loving only a man like Night Walker could offer. But there was more. She liked Night, admired his work ethic and dedication to his job, and re-spected his loyalty to her family. Plus, he was noth-ing like the young men she'd dated in college. They'd been immature, wanting only sex and her money.

She craved Night's calm, loved the way he could enter a room and fill it with power simply with his presence, the way he seemed unimpressed with the Langworthy fortune.

And she didn't give a damn what her daddy said, that it was beneath her to see the hired help, or that sleeping with him would spread gossip that might taint the great family name.

She simply wanted to feel Night's arms around her, have him teach her what it was like to be a woman, what it would be like to be possessed by someone primal and fearless and intensely sexy.

Downing the rest of her champagne, she reached

for another, then headed to the gazebo by the pond, her favorite spot on the estate. The guests slowly dwindled away, the midnight hour approaching. Curfew time for Cinderella.

Night would come looking for her soon.

If another agent was watching her, she would have hated the intrusion, but knowing Night's eyes were on her throughout the evening had been titillating.

As if he'd known all their heated encounters would lead to this moment, he stalled. She waited and watched him from the corner of her eye, but he didn't come to the gazebo. Finally, Holly finished off the champagne, certain he was intentionally trying to taunt her.

Then she saw him move from the shadows of the pond. He stood ramrod straight, his big hands shoved deep into the pockets of the dark suit he wore, the long black strands of his hair catching in the moonlight. He angled his head to check on her and she grinned, then sauntered toward him.

Her evening gown dipped low, exposing the gentle slope of her breasts. His eyes raked over her, and only the slightest tightening of his jaw gave away his desire. Then his gaze fastened onto her face.

"Don't you think it's time to turn in?"

"No." She wet her lips, no longer willing to deny how much she wanted him. She wasn't a child anymore. She had finished college. Was handling projects for her father's foundation now.

He took his time in speaking. He was definitely

not a talker, which made her even more curious about him. "Not tired?"

"Tired of waiting on you." Then she did what she'd desperately wanted to do all night—she reached up and slid her fingers into his hair.

His hands caught hers, wrapped around them in a tight grip. "Don't."

Holly licked her lips again, and buried her face against his chest. She was behaving shamelessly and she knew it. "I can't help it, Night. All I did during the party was think about you. About touching you."

She raised on tiptoe and pressed her lips to his, tracing her tongue around the edges, pleading for him to open. He didn't. He refrained, pushed her away, tried to right her dress by tugging up the top so he wouldn't be tempted by her cleavage. But she refused to give up.

Social status, their stations in life...the whole world be damned. She wanted Night and he wanted her. She had to make him see that nothing else mattered but the intense passion simmering between them.

With one flick of her hand, she released her hair from the diamond studded clip that had held it up, shaking the auburn tresses free. Desire swept over his features.

"You're playing with fire, Holly," he said in a gruff voice.

"I'm a big girl, Night. If I want to get burned, that's my choice."

His control seemed to snap, his patience evaporated. His stormy gaze trapped her with alarming intensity, the flare of his mouth sinful as he gripped her wrists and dragged her inside the gazebo. "*We can't do this, Holly.*"

"*Yes, we can.*" *Holly raked her nails across his chest.* "*I want you, Night. Nothing matters but the two of us. Not my father. Your job. It's just us.*" *She kissed his cheek, tracing her tongue along the edges of his mouth until she heard him groan.*

Still, he pulled back, stared at her for a heartbeat, heat radiating between them. She poured her love into her eyes, wanting him to see how much he had come to mean to her.

Then he suddenly jerked her into his embrace, pulling her against the hard wall of his chest and captured her mouth with his. "*This is wrong.*"

"*No,*" *she moaned.* "*I need you, Night, can't you see that?*"

As if her words had conjured the savage beast within him, he tore at her dress, slid it off her shoulders and traced a path along the nape of her neck to her breast, licking at the soft mounds.

Moaning, she threw her head back in wild abandon, ran her hands over his chest and lower to his sex. He hardened and pulsed against her. Wild with hunger, she stripped him while he suckled and bit at her neck until fire burned through her nerve endings. The sweet tingle of release seeped through her as she gazed in awe at his body. Dark skin stretched taut over rigid sculpted muscles, the sleek hairless sweat-soaked chest a reminder of his heritage. A half-cocked smile tilted his mouth when he noticed her gaze, then he rose above her, pushed her legs apart with his knees, buried his face in her hair, and claimed her.

It took him a second to realize that she was a virgin. His mouth tightened and he stared into her eyes, questions and accusations flaring. He started to pull away, but she cupped his hips in her hands and dragged him tighter, begging him to make her his—

A VOICE broke into the haze of her mind, and Holly jerked her eyes open, her heart pounding. She wanted to return to the safety of her dream, but reality intervened. She was lying on a cot in some kind of dingy room, cement walls, cement floor, not even a window.

And a crazed-looking man was stalking toward her with a needle.

THE TRACKING device Night had put on Holly's car had worked; she'd gone to the Langworthy cabin. A quick phone call to Night's associates and Colorado Confidential had dispatched a team to search the area.

But the news was disturbing. The horse Holly had ridden to the cabin was in the corral outside. Holly was nowhere to be seen. Scuff marks in the cabin and footsteps outside suggested she'd been assaulted. Other evidence indicated she'd been scuttled away in a helicopter, although the heavy snowfall had nearly obliterated the markings.

Colleen reported that she'd received a tip that Grace had holed up in some kind of laboratory fortress in the mountains for the past few years, somewhere between Ouray and Gunnison. No one could pinpoint the exact location, but they would have choppers scoping the area and would radio Night if they discovered it. More than likely, if Grace had Sky, the baby was hidden at the lab. Maybe he'd taken Holly there, too.

She never should have gone off alone. Why hadn't she phoned Night to go with her?

The terror in Celia's voice when she'd described Teddy Grace's behavior hammered fear into Night's chest, driving it deeper and deeper as he settled in for the chopper ride to Ouray.

If Grace had Holly and Schyler, what would he do with them?

"He'll probably keep the baby alive to test him," Celia had said in a weak voice. "But Holly—he might be abusive toward her, take his hatred for me out on her. He has a bad temper."

The memory of Night's last conversation with Holly flashed back. Holly was stubborn and independent. One reporter had written that she blamed herself for the kidnapping. Night hadn't helped with his condemning attitude either. Worse, her father had shut her out, had told her the feds were giving up, that she should give up. And Night had done no better; he hadn't been there to comfort her or to assure her that ICU wasn't giving up, that he wouldn't stop looking until he found their son.

He had to credit her for her bravery. Maybe she wasn't the spoiled girl he'd thought her to be.

The chopper cut over the snowcapped mountain peaks, the vast expanse of the countryside beautiful but dangerous, especially with the storm clouds raging around him. Newscasters had hinted of a blizzard, but Night had ignored the warning. He couldn't wait on another weather forecast.

The chopper shook, jerking up and down with the turbulence, and he braced himself for a bumpy ride. Once he got to the town, he'd rent a jeep, drive as far as he could into the San Juan mountains, and hike in on foot until he tracked down the laboratory.

He only prayed that Grace hadn't hurt Holly or his son.

Was Grace following through with the second part of his plan? If so, Holly Langworthy and her family would finally get what they deserved.

Especially since they had cheated him out of what he should have had.

He flexed his hands and stared at them, bitterness swelling inside. He had worked so hard, had sucked up to all the right people, had learned to play the political game just like the Langworthys. And he had come so close to having all his dreams come true.

They had been right at his fingertips, but the Langworthys had snapped them in two like they were nothing but cheap glass. But he would not break under the pressure of lost hopes.

Not like his own father had years ago.

Joshua Langworthy's face flashed onto the TV screen. Another interview. Another celebration of his good fortune. Another showing of the rich and famous Centennial family in their godlike glory.

But the new governor wouldn't be celebrating when he realized his baby sister was gone, and that his win had cemented her demise.

Chapter Three

The next time Holly woke, she felt stronger, her head clearer. She had no idea how long she'd been held prisoner, but as she surveyed her surroundings, she realized she was locked in some kind of cave-type room. The air was cold and dank, the floors and walls virtually made of stone as if they'd been carved out of the side of the mountain. She eased herself to an upright position, giving herself time to let the dizziness pass, then stumbled toward the door and banged on it.

"Let me out of here!" She yelled and slammed her fists against the surface, trying desperately to jiggle the knob free, but to no avail. Whoever had brought her here had her baby.

And she wanted to see him.

She pounded the door again, fighting tears of frustration. Finally she heard voices outside. Footsteps sounded, then faltered by the door, and the knob twisted. Fear squeezed her chest, but she braced herself, ready to fight her attacker if need be. Or beg, whichever would work most effectively.

She glanced quickly around for her purse and the gun, but her abductor had obviously confiscated it.

The door screeched open and a dark-haired man in his late thirties towered over her. She sized him up, deciding whether or not to fight him. He weighed at least fifty pounds more than she did, and his scathing green eyes warned her not to bother.

"Who are you? Do you have my son?"

He didn't speak. He simply seized her arm and dragged her through the doorway, down a long hallway supported by thick concrete columns, and through a maze of corridors. Cold air sucked at her lungs, disorienting her. "Where are you taking me? Who are you and where's my son?"

He ignored her, shoving her along, until he finally stopped at another room, unlocked the door and hauled her inside a laboratory. Test tubes, beakers, vials and medical equipment filled shelves above work counters housed with microscopes and other scientific equipment, and an assembly of test tubes filled with blood.

Holly's legs wobbled as he shoved her into a metal chair. "What am I doing here?"

The hulking man exited through a swinging door to a back room. Another man stepped through the cracks, this one older, mid-sixties, about five foot ten, with thinning white hair. His build was slight, but his serious demeanor and the crazed look in his eyes negated his slight size.

"Who are you and what have you done with my son?"

"I'm the man who should have been your father."

Holly stiffened. Theodore Grace—her mother's first husband? She'd seen pictures, but he'd been younger. Was it really him? Her mother claimed he was a madman, a crazed scientist who researched biological warfare.

"What do you want with me and my baby?"

"You'll understand everything, all in good time." His shoes clicked on the hard floor as he drew nearer, a hypodermic in his hand.

"Please don't drug me again," she pleaded. "Take me to my little boy."

The man's devilish eyes narrowed over thick glasses perched on his nose. "Yes, yes, I suppose that wouldn't hurt. But first, I must draw another blood sample."

"Why are you doing this? What could you possibly want with my blood?"

"To see what effects the virus you contracted months ago had on your body."

Holly bolted backward, determined to find an escape before this madman could touch her.

His nasty chuckle reverberated through the room. "There is no escape, not if you want to see your son." He paused, tapped the needle, waiting.

Holly froze. "Do you really have my baby?"

"Yes." He gestured toward the gurney. "If you fight me, I will have Bertram strap you down to the table. Or we can give you a sedative to knock you out again."

She cringed at the sight of the leather straps. No, she wouldn't let him tie her down or sedate her. She needed her wits about her to think. Realizing it was useless to fight, she relented, glaring at him as he drew the blood sample. When he finished, he gestured for her to stand and follow him. The other man, Bertram, reappeared and fell into step beside her, his menacing glare warning her not to try to escape. They veered down another corridor, which led to another. Holly tried to memorize her way, but the hallways all looked the same—rocky and cold, as if they were virtually isolated from the world. Then Bertram stopped at another door and unlocked it.

Holly gasped, her heart pounding as she entered the room. It was a nursery, painted a bright blue equipped with a crib, changing table, rocking chair and baby toys. An elderly nurse sat in the corner, rocking a baby in her arms. Oh, god! It was Schyler! She lurched forward, but the woman frowned up at her with suspicious eyes. The doctor gestured toward Holly. "Mary, let Miss Langworthy hold her son for a while."

Her breath caught. The nurse's air of possessiveness toward Holly's son was as frightening as the crazed scientist. But Mary did as she was instructed.

Tears swam in Holly's eyes, and her heart squeezed as she cradled her son back into her arms, where he belonged.

NIGHT HAD BEEN tracking through the mountains for almost two days, climbing the rocky terrain between Ouray and Gunnison, weaving in and out of the tall Ponderosa pines and spruce trees, and peering down at mile after mile of untouched, brown-hued hillsides. Colleen had wanted him to wait for backup, but he'd insisted they couldn't waste time. He'd promised to radio his location when he found the lab so that she could helicopter in help.

He had had no sleep and had stopped only long enough for water as he made his way through the gorges and canyons. Before he had started on the journey, he had gathered natural herbs, roots and berries to create one of the ancestral potions he had been taught by his grandfather, then built a fire, stripped his shirt, and drank the concoction, calling upon his native soul as he always did before a mission. In the tradition of the Cheyenne warrior, he had chanted and prayed, remembering the words he had learned as a young boy.

The scent is in your blood. You are a horse whisperer, the grandson of a mighty Cheyenne. Become one with the land and earth that gave you life, and follow your instincts.

During the grueling hours he climbed and tracked through the wilderness, he allowed the peace of the land to drive him and calm the inner turmoil threatening to destroy his concentration. When he came upon a cave, he left firewood, provisions as well as a backpack of baby supplies inside, in case he and Holly needed shelter on the return trip to his jeep.

When he had first seen Holly, he had given her the name Laughing Green Eyes, because she radiated life and joy, and the Cheyenne believed in rejoicing in life. He had nearly fallen in love at the sight of her, but had convinced himself he was simply in lust. He had been alone so long. Had always felt isolated from the world. Had known that his future was not destined for love or family. That walking the tightrope between the old ways of his people and the modern white man's world made it impossible for him to really belong.

Her youthful exuberance, her excitement over the smallest moments in her daily life, had drawn her to him. She had been a feather of a free spirit, replacing the brashness of reality from his soul with her sweetness.

Yet, the last time he'd seen her, there had been no laughter in her eyes.

She had changed, had grown up, had suffered during the past few months. Remorse knotted his stomach. He had felt guilty for destroying her innocence that night, for crossing the line between employer and employee. His job had become his life. He had nothing else.

And he couldn't allow himself to believe that a beautiful, young woman as Holly would want more from a jaded half breed like himself than one night. In fact, he was sure her seduction was an act of rebellion against her father, a game he had more sense than to play. He'd learned a hard lesson with another rich girl, Charity Carmichael.

Charity had welcomed his attention, had warmed his bed at night, then when her father had discovered they were lovers, she had betrayed him in the worst way—she'd claimed he had tried to force himself on her. Night had never forgotten the shame he had felt with her accusations. The beating that had followed. The realization that he had been a fool to drink from the pool of water on the opposite side of the tracks.

The very reason he'd known nothing could happen between him and Holly.

Would things have been different if he'd disagreed with her father about the two of them belonging together? Would Holly have married him and allowed him to be a father to their child? Or had she simply wanted to taste his passion, as Charity had done? Once Holly had had her fill, would she, like Charity, have decided that a blue-blooded man made better husband material than one filled with red blood?

He couldn't forget that Holly had not even tried to find him, not once during the nine months of her pregnancy, or when their baby had been born, or in the months since.

When his thoughts turned to grief over the lost months with his child, he called upon the Cheyenne beliefs again—the golden thread of Cheyenne existence—not to long for the past, but to rejoice in the present.

He would channel his anger and pain into the hunt.

And when he found his son, he would share the stories of the Sun dance and the Big Dipper and the Seven Stars with him. He would teach his son the traditions of their proud people. Even if Holly or her father tried to deny him.

Memories of life on the reservation crowded his mind. The difficulty his white mother had had fitting in, the isolation he'd felt being part of two worlds, but not belonging to either. Did he want his boy to suffer the same fate?

His radio beeped, and he answered, hoping Colorado Confidential had news.

"Night, it's Colleen. Listen, Wiley found something in Helio's effects.'' She paused. ''We believe Grace has built a lab in a cave.''

''Do you know the location?''

She gave him the coordinates.

''Thanks, I'm not too far from there. I'll check it out.''

By the time Night reached the area Colleen had mentioned, the sun was setting, a gray misty fog enveloping the canyon below. He finally spotted a strange rock formation that jutted out from the side of the mountain. Shrouded in heavy brush and trees and snow, it was hardly visible from his viewpoint. Not visible at all from the sky.

He checked his compass, noting the coordinates. Could this be the cave housing Grace's fortress?

He sped up, running up the steep incline, taking the jagged rock ledges as if they were stair steps. Snow crunched beneath his feet, but he measured his footsteps, padding silently across the ice as he approached the mouth of the cave. Before he went in, he phoned in his location to Colorado Confidential. ''I think I've located it.''

''Wait for backup,'' Colleen ordered.

''I'm just going to check it out, see if Holly or the baby is here.''

''Night, wait—''

He cut the connection. He had no intention of giving Grace more time to hurt Holly or his son.

Moving closer, he listened for signs of a guard, the chant of his people's Sundance echoing in the foothills of his mind. Pine-crested hills and thick Douglas firs and pinions cradled the formation in their depths, scrub brush and trees nearly covering the entrance. He moved forward, pushing through the dense brush, checking the parameter for another doorway. He had to make his entrance unannounced. Thankfully, Grace had not installed high-tech security. He obviously thought his fortress so isolated it would never be detected.

To the east, he located a side door buried beneath the snow-capped vegetation, and managed to open the door. He waited for an alarm to sound, but heard nothing. Still, Grace might have a system that activated a silent alarm, so he paused to listen for the sounds of men approaching before he continued. Giving his eyes time to adjust to the grayness of the interior, he allowed his senses to drive him through the corridors. He had to find Holly and baby Schyler and make certain they were safe.

Then he would deal with Theodore Grace.

HOLLY HAD MISSED precious moments with her son, had worried she might not even recognize him, but one look into his brown eyes and she realized she would always have a connection to him—and to his father.

Schyler had grown so much. His little hands and cheeks were now pudgy, as was his face. He was able to hold his head up, and sit up by himself. Her heart squeezed.

She had missed seeing him learn to do that.

He swatted at her hands playfully, his dark eyes searching her face. Did he recognize her? Remember her scent?

She sniffed the blanket wrapped around him, then

his hair—he carried a faint odor that reminded her of Night. Then she traced a finger over the crown of his head, the fine hair which was now thicker and even darker than it had been at birth. It had grown, too. So had his little fingernails. And he had developed chubby little rolls around his legs, and dimples in his cheeks....

Wiping away tears, she recognized Night's soulful, serious expression in those eyes. Schyler had the same stubborn thrust of his chin and high cheekbones as his father. And his thick dark hair reminded her of the man she had thought she had loved. The man she still craved. All these months, even after he had deserted her, she had wanted him, had imagined what it might be like for her and Night to raise their child together.

Where was he now? Did he know she had come looking for their son? Was he out there somewhere, searching for them?

Sky whimpered, and she traced a finger over his hand, cuddling him in the blanket. "Hey, little guy. Did you miss me? I'm your Mommy, remember?"

He cooed and clasped her hand with his fingers.

"Are you all right? That doctor didn't hurt you, did he?"

The short, stocky woman pressed her thin lips together into a tight line. "Of course Dr. Grace didn't hurt him. And I love babies. I take good care of him."

Although the woman's icy green eyes held no hint of friendliness, Holly forced herself to thank her. "I'm glad. I've been so worried about him."

"Dr. Grace means him no harm. But he needs the boy for his research."

Holly frowned. "What research?"

"It's not my job to tell." She set about tidying the nursery at a brisk pace.

The nurse obviously didn't intend to talk further, so Holly focused on enjoying the time with her baby. She examined his feet, his hands, his face, cooing and talking to him, telling him how much she missed him and loved him. "We'll never be apart again," she whispered, earning another evil look from Mary.

Finally, when Sky yawned and his eyes began to drift closed with fatigue, she sang the lullaby she'd sung to him when she'd brought him home from the hospital. Did he remember her or had he begun to think of the old woman as his mother? He was seven months old now, had he started to babble? Had he called the nurse Mama?

As if to answer her and quiet her worries, Schyler snuggled to her, sucking on his thumb, and drifted back to sleep. But other questions bombarded her, all the things she should know about her own child but had lost. Was he eating baby food now? Did he like peas or fruit? Bananas or pears? Had he started to teethe?

Mary walked over and reached for Schyler.

"Please let me stay and tend to him," Holly said, tightening her grip. "And will you get the bunny in my bag for him—it was his favorite toy." Sky startled and began to fuss. Holly rocked him back and forth, but Mary ignored Holly's plea, and snapped her fingers. Bertram suddenly appeared.

"He must sleep," Mary said. "And you must go now."

"But—" Holly's protests died on her lips as Mary removed the baby. "Please give him his toy bunny." She reached for him again, but Bertram snatched her arm, then pushed her outside into the corridor. Holly wanted to cry out for her son, but she didn't want to frighten him. Still, as Bertram dragged her along the maze of corridors and her son grew farther away, panic seized her.

"When can I see him again?"

Bertram ignored her, his fingers biting into her already bruised skin.

"Tell me, damn it. Why can't I stay with my son?"

He shook her as if she were a rag doll. "Be quiet."

"You have no right to do this." Anger mushroomed. What if they didn't let her see her son again? "Let me go! I want to stay with my baby!"

He gripped her chin so tightly she gasped in pain, unlocking the door with his free hand. "Get inside, Miss Langworthy."

Holly kicked Bertram's shin and tried to run, but he jerked her arm behind her back and twisted it so hard she yelped with pain. "If you want a chance to visit your baby again, then cooperate."

Pain sliced through her shoulder. She felt as if he was tearing her arm out of the socket. Then he shoved her inside the room, and locked it behind him. She fell on the concrete, cradling her arm to soothe the pain.

Tears clouded her vision. She crawled back to the

door and beat on the metal until she was so exhausted and hoarse, she trembled with fatigue. Frustrated and already aching for her son again, she finally crawled onto the cot, then rolled into a fetal position, giving in to despair and letting the tears fall. She had no idea where this madman had brought her and her baby.

How would Night or the other detectives ever find them?

NIGHT STOOD in the shadows of the cave on the opposite side and watched the scene, his gut tightening. At least Holly was still alive. If he had entertained the idea that she had helped stage the kidnapping, he was certain that idea was false. He'd heard the anguish in her sobs as she'd been tossed into the room alone.

Thank God she was a fighter. They both would have to stay strong to rescue his son.

He searched the darkness in case the big man returned, waiting several minutes before he picked the lock and snuck inside the room.

Holly lay on the dirty cot, curled into a ball, sobs wrenching from her. At the sight of her anguish, the fury he'd felt at Holly for denying him knowledge of his son dissipated slightly. He padded toward her, his footsteps so silent that she didn't hear him until he slid down on the bed beside her. She startled then, cried out, and rolled over to fight him. He covered her mouth with his hand and captured her hands above her head, pinning her to the bed. She struggled and tried to knee him in the groin, but he forced her to look up at him.

''Shh, look at me, Holly. Quiet now.''

Her green eyes widened, the orbs sparkling with tears. Then recognition dawned, and she nodded, her relief palpable in the way she relaxed. Still, the depth of the sadness in her expression was so strong that Night couldn't help himself—he pulled her into his arms and cradled her against him.

HOLLY HAD NEVER been so grateful to see anyone in her entire life. She sank into Night's arms, memories of the last time he had held her stirring, along with the feelings she had forced at bay the last time they had spoken. She knew Night hated her, would never forgive her for keeping Sky's birth a secret, that he blamed her for not protecting their child, but at least he had come. He would rescue their son.

She tried to stem the tears and calm herself, but the last few hours drove the nightmare of their situation home. Night stroked her back, the soft purr of his breath against her hair a reminder that she wasn't alone anymore. Night was here, he would save them.

She trusted him with every fiber of her being, had trusted him the first time they had met.

His big hands slowed, moved to her face, then he gently eased her tangled hair from her cheek and tilted her head back to look at her. ''Are you all right? Did he hurt you?''

His words were a mere whisper in the cave of a room.

''I'm okay…I saw our baby.''

He froze, his hands tightening around her face. ''Is he all right?''

"Yes…" her voice broke. "He's beautiful, even more beautiful than I remembered."

A ghost of a smile greeted her, sending a dozen sensations rippling through her. Sensations she had no business feeling for a man who had walked away from her when she had needed him most. Sensations she couldn't act upon now, not when their lives and their baby's life depended on quick action.

As if he suddenly realized the compromising position they were in, that defenses had fled and that he was still holding her, that she desperately wanted the comfort of his kiss, he suddenly pulled away.

Footsteps echoed outside the hall. Night pressed a finger to her lips, then slid soundlessly to the floor and flattened himself against the wall behind the door.

Tension rippled through the room as they waited.

Chapter Four

Night pressed himself against the wall, preparing to battle whoever stepped through the doorway, but the footsteps clicked past and continued down the hall, the voices fading. He remained in hiding for several more seconds until he sensed they were in the clear, then returned to the cot beside Holly. Her green eyes were red-rimmed and swollen, her face pale, but she was still beautiful. The realization that he had almost kissed her earlier rocked him to the core.

Apparently, she still possessed the power to rob him of rational thought.

But they didn't have time to explore those feelings. They had to escape and rescue their baby.

"How did you find me?" Holly asked.

"It's a long story," Night whispered, remembering that her father hadn't shared the details of the case with her. "The trace evidence left in Sky's nursery was linked to a Merino sheep ranch partially owned by Senator Franklin Gettys. Your cousin, Conrad Burke, connected the senator to mobster Helio DeMarco. DeMarco and Dr. Grace also have a connection."

Holly shivered. "I met Teddy Grace earlier. He's just as crazy as Mom said."

Night nodded.

"But I don't understand why he wants me or Sky. Is he trying to punish my mother and father because Mom divorced him and married Dad?"

"Revenge almost definitely played into his game plan," Night said. "But he has a bigger agenda. Do you remember the flu that struck Silver Rapids a few months ago?"

"Yes. I was sick then myself. It was while I was pregnant."

"Right." He imagined her round with his child and his heart squeezed. He wished he could have seen her.

"Grace orchestrated your trip to Silver Rapids. Helio convinced his nephew, Tony, to trick Marilyn into getting you there so that you would be exposed to the germ."

"Oh, my God. Did Marilyn know?"

"No, and she was horrified when she learned she'd had a part in it." He studied her for a moment, wondering if she was strong enough to hear the rest. But, he had no choice. He saw the wheels spinning in her head and knew she was putting it all together.

"Does that mean that I passed on this germ to Sky?"

She looked so frail he reached out to rub her arms. "Yes, but no one knows the effect it might have. We suspect that's Grace's motive for kidnapping Sky. He wants to keep him here for testing."

Holly's face turned ashen. "That's the reason he drew blood from me."

Night's lips pressed into a flat line. "Apparently Grace infected your cousin Con with a germ when he was little. Con was sick at the time, so the germ worked in reverse to boost his immune system." He forced a smile, although he knew it was stiff. "Con says he hasn't been sick a day since."

Panic darkened her eyes. "But Sky is healthy. Does that mean he'll get sick from the virus?"

"We don't know yet, but if he were going to be ill, chances are he probably would have contracted something by now."

Holly nodded, although her lower lip trembled as she looked up at him. He wanted to offer more but he couldn't. Not until they had some answers.

She reached out and took his hand, played with his fingers. "Night, I'm…so sorry about not telling you about Sky. I…I wanted to."

He inhaled sharply, struggling not to let her admission affect him, but the sincerity lacing her voice hacked away at his anger, chipping away the top layer. He wished he could tell her it was all right, but it wasn't. They would have to work out their personal issues later.

He pulled away and stood, ignoring the wince on her face at his withdrawal. Instead, he focused on his plan. "We need to find Sky and get out of here. Are you ready?"

HOLLY CUT her gaze around the cold dank room and nodded. There was so much more she wanted to say, but she would have to wait. At least they were working together to save their son.

''Can you take me to the room where they're holding Sky?''

Holly shrugged. ''I'm not sure. We wound through a lot of hallways.''

''Don't worry, we'll find him.'' He squeezed her hand. ''I can get us back to the side door where I came in. I heard you in the hallway with your guard when I entered, so I can probably sense the direction from there.''

''That's Bertram.'' She shivered. Holly knew Night was trying to reassure her, and appreciated his calm demeanor. She breathed easier as he opened the door a crack and paused to search the darkened interior of the corridor. She noticed the gun tucked into the waistband of his jeans. As they moved out, his footsteps were so quiet they were nonexistent while hers seemed to echo in the hollow hallway. She latched onto his hand and followed. Mildew and must permeated the air. Water trickled somewhere in the distance. A skittering sound, like mice, made her pause.

He pointed to the left at the first corner. Again, she remembered the aura of mystery that had drawn her to Night before, and admired his ability to home in on his instincts.

They crept along the concrete floor, twisting and turning and weaving through the maze until frustration pulled at Holly. She tried to remember the series of turns Bertram had taken her on, but she had been dizzy with fear and hadn't acclimated to the darkness. Night held up his finger, signaling her to stop, and Holly recognized the trickle of water running down the inside of the cave. "That way," he mouthed.

She nodded, faintly remembering hearing the sound before, too. They passed several locked doorways that appeared to be labs. Night slowly eased by them, peering through the small square window at the top of the doorway, each time shaking his head to indicate he saw no one inside.

A strange screeching sound echoed from down the hallway, and Night motioned that he wanted to check it out. "If we find the details of Grace's research, maybe we'll know what we're up against with the germ tests that he gave you and Schyler," he whispered.

Holly nodded, deciding the sounds were animals. What in the world was Dr. Grace doing to them?

Night opened the door and they crept inside. The counter was filled with standard lab equipment, microscopes, test tubes, quick-freeze dryers, centrifuges and eggs.

"Another lab," Night whispered. "I'm going to look around." Holly stood guard at the door while he explored the laboratory counters and scrounged through some of the files on the desk. "He was working on recombinant and gene therapy techniques," Night explained as he scanned the files. "He's been infecting bacteria with viruses to change the bacterial DNA and make new strains of bacteria."

"But why?" Holly asked.

"He wants to transfer this technique to infect other living things with viruses that help boost the immune system instead of destroying it. This sounds like the method he used on Con. But to earn money, he also created and sold germs and bacteria to Helio, the mobster I told you about. Helio used them on his enemies.''

"So, the weird growths in those petri dishes could potentially be very dangerous?'' Holly asked.

"Exactly.'' The screeching animal sounds grew louder, reverberating in the lab through a connecting back room door. Night went to check it out. Seconds later, he motioned for Holly to come and see for herself.

Holly froze in the doorway, covering her mouth with her hand to stifle a gasp. Rows and rows of cages lined the room, filled with mice, birds, chimpanzees. "Is he testing his viruses on all those animals?''

"Some.'' Night scanned the charts attached to a few of the cage fronts. "He's also doing cloning experiments. Trying to use animal stem cells to compare to human embryonic ones. Our theory is that, through Helio DeMarco, he was culturing bacteria for bio warfare, then testing the germs on the unsuspecting public.''

Night headed back to the front laboratory room, grabbed a chair and began tapping into the computer. Holly followed, leaning over his shoulder to study the information as it spilled onto the screen.

"Here are notes on the Silver Rapids flu,'' Night said. "Grace is definitely responsible for the Q fever. Apparently it was the Q fever microbe that caused the people to get sick, not the virus.''

"I don't understand all this,'' Holly said.

"It's pretty technical, but the gist is that he's

playing with fire, and people's lives," Night said.
"There are files on other cases, too. Apparently he's
been testing his germs in other parts of the country
as well."

"He's a monster," Holly said. "And doing it to
innocent people."

Night's gaze met hers, their thoughts obviously
in synch. Grace had no conscience. He was even
experimenting on children, like their son.

From the back room, the birds squawked louder
and the other animals screeched wildly. Night
pressed his finger to her lip, then pointed to the connecting room, indicating a door which opened to the
hallway. Someone was unlocking it to check on the
animals. He pulled Holly down beside the desk.
They crawled along the edges, hiding behind the
other desks and equipment until they reached the
front lab door.

But just as they stood to escape, Dr. Grace strode
through the doorway with a pistol in his hand, aimed
at them.

Night coaxed Holly behind him, trying to protect
her with his body as they stood and faced the man
he presumed was Teddy Grace.

"Well, well. I've been expecting you, Walker."
Grace gestured toward the gun at Night's waistband.
"Drop the gun on the floor and kick it over here."

Damn it. Night hated to relinquish his weapon,
but he had no choice. He couldn't take a chance on
getting Holly killed. He slowly slid his hand to his
pants, removed the Glock and dropped it on the li-
noleum. He gave it a gentle kick, not quite close

enough for Grace to reach without having to move. When Grace bent to retrieve it, Night would attack.

But Grace was smarter than he'd hoped. He motioned for Bertram, who'd entered the connecting back lab room where the animals were kept, to pick it up. Bertram did so quickly, then joined his boss.

A bold sneer twisted Grace's face. "So, what do you think of my lab?"

"That the government would be interested in your work," Night said. Holly tensed behind him, and he forced his voice to remain steady.

"I've tried that route before," Grace said in a cynical tone. "The government didn't appreciate my efforts the way they should have."

"No, even the government has some scruples about unleashing dangerous germs on innocent people."

Grace shrugged. "A few must be sacrificed for the good of mankind."

"What you're doing isn't good, it's evil," Holly said.

Harsh laughter echoed across the room. "I beg to differ. Some of my germ tests may prove that bio engineering can offer immunity to disease. I might save the world from HIV or cancer."

"But you'll kill how many people before you perfect it? If you ever do." Night cleared his throat. "And what about the germ you exposed our son to?"

"In case you haven't figured it out, that's the reason you're here." Grace gestured toward the gurney. "Now, I have samples of Miss Langworthy's blood. I need some of yours, Walker."

Night swallowed. "What for?"

"To compare your blood to your baby's."

"What are you looking for?" Night asked.

"I'll check all the genetic components, study the interactions, and differences between your blood, Miss Langworthy's and the baby's."

Night frowned. "Tell me about the germ you exposed my son to."

"It was a combination of a retrovirus and Q fever. The retrovirus shouldn't affect adults, but my hope is that it is carried to the unborn baby through the mother's bloodstream. If my hypothesis is correct, it will enhance his immune system."

"This is the same virus that was included in the Q fever germ spray you sprayed in Silver Rapids. So, you don't know for sure that it will have positive effects?"

Grace smiled shrewdly. "You're finally catching on, Walker. The reason for testing your son."

"Did Senator Gettys know what you were doing?" Night asked.

Grace laughed. "He thought they were testing the vaccine spray to see how the spray mist and sprayers worked."

"But you don't know what the results will be," Holly said, emotion hardening her voice. "You might have exposed my baby to something deadly."

Night grit his teeth. "Then he didn't know you and Helio were using a live version of the bug?"

"No." Grace shrugged.

"You'll never get away with this," Night said.

More laughter from Grace followed. "You're wrong. No one will track you down here."

"Don't be so sure," Night said. "Agents are on their way now. They have the coordinates."

"Yes, but with the impending blizzard, they'll never be able to see the lab from the sky. And they won't reach us before we escape."

Night heard Holly's sharp intake of air and silently willed her not to panic. Although their situation seemed bleak, he would find a way to get them free.

After that, he had no idea what would happen.

HOLLY WATCHED in disgust while Grace tightened the tourniquet around Night's muscular arm, then inserted the needle to draw blood. Night sat stone straight, expressionless as he stared at the doctor, his menacing glare unnerving her, but not deterring the doctor in his mission.

"When you finish, can we see our baby?" Holly asked.

Grace glanced up from the needle and shrugged. "I suppose it won't hurt for you to be together while you're here."

Relief surged through Holly. Night's mouth twitched slightly, the only sign that he cared one way or the other. He wore a mask over his emotions, she realized, a protective measure against the pain. But he must feel deeply.

She dragged her gaze away from the blood seeping into the test tube. She had never mastered such control and wore her feelings on her sleeve. The reason she'd been an easy target for men to take advantage of when she was younger. She'd been starry eyed and romantic, so sure that every man she dated would fall in love with her, when they had simply been in love with her money. Her father had tried to warn her.

But then he'd partnered with Carlton Sanders.

Another incident that had come between them. But at least she knew now that her father hadn't orchestrated Sky's kidnapping. Her parents must be out of their minds with worry.

The sound of Night's feet hitting the floor as he shoved himself off the gurney broke her thoughts.

"Let's go." Grace and Bertram both aimed their guns at chest level and nudged her forward. Night sent her a silent message, his eyes urging her to do as they said. She offered him a small smile to let him know she understood, that she wouldn't do anything to jeopardize the rescue of their child.

NIGHT MEMORIZED the way as Grace and his crony escorted them to the nursery. In spite of his ability to maintain his mask of calm, his heart was pounding inside his chest. After four long months of searching for his son, he was finally going to meet him. A quiver of apprehension snaked through him. Would his little boy connect with him?

Yes.

The ways of his people ran deep in the blood. His son would look into his eyes and know. Night had to keep his faith in all things eternally true to his nature.

He instinctively knew when they neared the nursery. His son's cry rang through the halls. Holly's eyes shifted to his, anxiety sparking in the depths. He focused on remaining calm, hoping to reassure her.

You are a horse whisperer. Read the signs. Speak to the vulnerable one's fears.

He had to do the same for his son and his son's mother.

Bertram unlocked the door and he allowed Holly to enter first. She hurried toward a nurse, who was pacing the floor with the screaming infant.

"Here, let me have him," Holly said.

The woman sidestepped her and continued her shushing, bouncing Schyler up in the air in frantic jerky movements.

"You're scaring him," Holly said. "Give me my baby."

Night stilled beside the crib, his gaze locked onto the squirming little boy. Did he sense the strife in the room? Realize he had been torn from the bosom of his mother and thrust into the unknown? Into the clutches of a madman?

The nurse tightened her grip. "He doesn't know her." She directed her shrill comment to Grace. "She is not fit to be his mother."

The sound of anguish Holly emitted felt like a punch to Night's stomach, yet he checked his reaction.

"Give her the child, Mary," Grace commanded.

Mary backed away but Bertram placed a hand on her back. "Yes, Mary, give the baby to the woman. For now."

A sinister look crossed Mary's face but she finally relented. Holly eagerly accepted Sky into her arms, her eyes lighting up with such affection as she gazed down at their son that Night moved nearer.

Footsteps echoed behind him, then the door clicked shut, locking them inside.

Night reached a finger out to ease back the baby blanket and get his first real look at his son. Pride swelled in his chest, a smile soaring through him.

His son was perfect. He had olive skin, eyes the color of Night's grandfather North, and prominent features that announced his heritage.

Sky whimpered, his fists circling in agitation. "Shh, honey, it's okay, Mommy's here." Tears shimmered in Holly's eyes as she cooed and whispered nonsensical baby talk.

Then she leaned over and planted a kiss on the baby's forehead. "I love you, sweetheart. Now, there's somebody very important you need to meet."

With tears in her eyes, Holly angled the baby to look up at him. "Schyler, this is your father. He's come to take us home."

Chapter Five

Holly's stomach tightened as she placed her son in his father's arms. During those long months of pregnancy, she'd lain in bed at night, so alone, dreaming about how different things might be if she and Night had been together. If he had loved her. But her father had convinced her that Night would not want to be burdened with her or their child.

Yet the undisguised love in his eyes as he cuddled Schyler against his big chest proved she had been wrong about the second part.

And she had been wrong to keep the baby from him, even if he wanted no part of her. No matter what her father said, no matter that when he had confronted Night about the two of them sleeping together, Night had claimed he'd only wanted sex from her, that he wanted nothing more to do with her, she had known in her heart it was wrong to keep a lie.

Only she had been afraid.

Afraid of her father's wrath. Afraid of embarrassing the great Centennial family. Afraid of Night's condemnation, that he might think she had purposely gotten pregnant to trick him into marriage.

And even more afraid that he might love the baby, but not her.

Shame filled her for being so selfish and immature.

Baby Sky needed his father. He deserved to know his roots, his heritage and the man who possessed her heart. Even if he had hurt her unbearably and made her want to close herself off from love forever.

Night gently rocked their baby back and forth in his arms, his husky voice murmuring words in his ancient language, words she didn't understand but that seemed to soothe her son. Schyler turned his big, chocolate-brown eyes up to his father, studying Night's face as if he sensed a deep-rooted connection. "When we get out of here, my son, I will tell you stories of our people. Stories of the Buffalo ceremony, of the Sacred Arrows, of the Crows." Then for the first time in his life, or at least since Holly had been with him, Sky began to coo and babble. Precious little sounds that warmed her heart and brought a rare smile to Night's lips.

"He understands that we are his parents," Night said in a gruff tone.

"I..." Holly tucked the blanket around her son's sock-clad feet. "I was so afraid he'd forget me."

Night looked up at her for the first time since he had taken his baby in his arms. "As Sweet Medicine, the cultural hero of the Cheyenne tribe, once said, there is a special power about women. They are the bringers of life to the people and the teachers of the little children.'' He paused, his dark eyes intense. ''A little boy can never forget his mama.''

The sincerity of his words tugged at Holly's already raw emotions. She had never heard him talk about his heritage. It was almost as if he were two different people. The tough, mysterious detective. The wise, powerful Native American.

She wanted to know more about both.

And although it pained her to admit it, she had to be honest. Seeing the stark resemblance between father and son cemented the realization. ''He needs his father, too.''

His gaze locked with hers, his expression unreadable, a strained heartbeat of silence passing before he turned his attention back to their son.

Yes, it was obvious Night wanted his little boy, but not her. She only hoped that if they escaped and everyone survived, that Night wouldn't try to take Schyler away from her. As a detective, he certainly had the power and means at his disposal. And if he disappeared to one of the reservations in Colorado or Montana and enlisted his people to hide his baby, she'd never be able to find him.

A SON NEEDS HIS FATHER.

Night stared at his little boy's sleeping form and fought the swell of emotions bombarding him. At least Holly had admitted that much. But would she remember her admission once they escaped and made it back to the Langworthy mansion? Would she stand up to the Langworthys if they protested letting Night be a part of his son's life?

And what about Holly? Did *she* need him?

Or would she return to the arms of Carlton Sanders? Would she marry the up-and-coming politician and allow the man to be a father to Sky, then force Night to play the drop-in parent?

How exactly did she feel about Sanders?

He stemmed the onslaught of questions, refusing to travel that road. He was not getting involved with Holly again, not in any way except to coordinate visits to see Schyler. His reasons for thinking the two of them didn't belong together hadn't changed since he'd first met her, and he didn't see any way they could change. She had used him much as Charity Carmichael had, then dismissed him when a richer guy came along. Not that Samuel Langworthy had beaten him to a pulp the way Mr. Carmichael had had his hired hands do, but his verbal threats had been just as menacing. Langworthy had threatened to disown Holly. He could never have torn her from the world she'd grown up in, denied her her parents and home. Even if Colleen had stood by Holly, it would devastate her to lose her father.

And eventually she might blame him.

You have a son now.

That son changed everything. He wasn't alone in the world now.

But wasn't he?

His son belonged to the Langworthys, carried their name…

"What do you think Dr. Grace is going to do to us?" Holly asked.

Night winced inwardly. He knew the answer, but the harsh reality might trigger panic.

"He'll kill us, won't he?"

He searched her face, but found courage in her determined green eyes, the trace of fear almost hidden. Admiration for the way she was handling the situation mounted in his chest.

"Probably, once he's finished his testing and doesn't need us anymore."

She bit down on her lower lip. "What…about Sky?"

His expression softened. "I think he wants to see the long-term effects on our son."

Relief surged out through her sigh. "So, he doesn't plan to kill him?"

"I don't think so." He traced a finger over the baby's foot. "But he will use him like a lab rat."

Pain flickered in her eyes, but she jutted up her chin. "We have to stop him."

"I know." He needed his lock pick, his gun. Thank goodness he'd hidden the backpack of supplies outside and he'd brought along formula and diapers. They'd need them on the long hike back to the jeep.

Holly wrapped her arms around her midriff, and he sensed she needed to hold the baby again, so he brushed his lips across the soft skin of his son's cheek, then gently eased the bundle into her outstretched arms. The expression on her face transformed from fear to love in a second, the protective flare in her eyes so motherly that he reconfirmed his vow to see that mother and child escaped safely.

He paced across the room, examining the door, then the small adjoining room which housed a bathroom and a cot where the nurse had slept at night. "We need to formulate a plan."

Holly nodded and sat down in the rocking chair, slowly rocking Sky back and forth. "I hope you have one in mind."

"When Bertram or Grace returns, follow my lead. I'll try to convince Grace to open up about the lab work, maybe show us around. When I see an opening, I'll attack, then we'll make a run for it."

Holly raised Sky to her shoulder and patted his back. "You won't take any chances that he'll hurt Sky?"

Her question rankled him. How could she even ask? "Of course not. How did Grace get you here, Holly? Does he have a four-wheel drive hidden somewhere?"

Holly closed her eyes and tried to remember the details. "A helicopter, I think. I saw one flying over the Aspen cabin when I arrived, but thought it was one of those rescue ones. Anyway, when I arrived at the family cabin, I didn't see any cars, so I thought no one was there. I was wrong." She hesitated, remembering her fear. "Someone was hiding inside. I saw a shadow move and reached for my pistol, but a man jumped me. He put a chloroformed rag over my face. Before I passed out, I heard the helicopter again."

Night scraped a hand through his hair, pulling it back into its leather thong. "He must have a hidden landing pad, but I didn't see it when I approached."

"How did you get here?"

"ICU dropped me outside Ouray. I took a jeep as far as I could, then hiked through the mountains. But if we could reach Grace's helicopter, we could make a faster escape."

"I have no idea where it's kept. When I woke up, I was lying in that room where you found me."

Night nodded. "Maybe we can get Grace to slip up and tell us."

"Do the other agents know where we are?" Holly asked. "Are they looking for us?"

"I radioed the location, but it'll take time." At Holly's imploring look, he realized it was time for more truths. "Holly, there are others searching for us. Actually, ICU is part of a larger, secret group called Colorado Confidential. They work for the government." He hesitated. "I work for them now, using ICU as a cover. Your parents don't even know about Colorado Confidential. They're based on a ranch called the Royal Flush. I work as a horse trainer there as my cover."

Her eyes widened. "That's why I couldn't find you."

"Yes." That and her father, but he didn't want to hurt her by telling her that.

"But like Grace said, it's hard to spot from the air, and they can't land nearby. It might take days."

Days they didn't have. Days in which Grace might snap and kill them, or decide to experiment with another germ on one of them. One that might have side effects even worse than death....

She sighed, and he noticed the dark circles beneath her eyes, the way her limbs sagged with fatigue. She didn't look strong enough to travel.

"You should probably get some sleep," he said. "You're going to need your rest if we're forced to set out on foot."

Holly glanced down at Sky and chewed on her

lip. "He'll be all right, Holly. But the stronger you are, the better chance we have of getting away and surviving. The elements can be brutal this time of year."

"I don't think I can sleep." She stared at him for a long moment, the wariness in her eyes stealing her earlier bravado. "I just hate to let him go now. Even for a second."

In spite of his resolve to remain unaffected by her, the catch in her voice twisted his insides. He braced himself against his own feelings. He would do whatever was necessary to free them. "Come on, it's important you try. Our son is going to need you to be strong."

His words seemed to convince her, and she relented, allowing him to help her stand. His throat closed as he watched her place Sky in the crib and cover him up. "There's Bun-Bun, Sky." She spotted the stuffed bunny in the corner and placed it close to Sky, then lingered for several seconds, staring at their baby.

He couldn't help but reach out and touch her, stroke her back. "Thank you, Holly. You have given me a beautiful boy," he said in a throaty voice.

She glanced up at him and smiled, though tears pooled in her eyes. "He is beautiful."

Moved by her emotions, he led her to the cot and coaxed her to lie down.

"Go to sleep now. I'll watch over our son." For a brief second, he allowed himself to imagine that they were past this nightmare.

But even if they survived, there would be other

challenges. Holly's family. Society. His job. Although times had changed somewhat, learning to be a Cheyenne and fit into a white man's world would not be easy for his son. Would belonging to the Langworthy family make his life easier or more difficult? "Rest, Holly. Sleep while Schyler sleeps."

"Thank you for coming," Holly said softly. Then fatigue must have overcome her, because she closed her eyes.

He walked away before he did something stupid like lie down beside her and hold her in his arms. If he touched her right now, he would want her. Not just once this time. But over and over. She was his son's mother, his former lover.

But becoming involved with Holly would be a mistake. He absolutely couldn't take her to his bed again or let her inside his heart. Holly obviously didn't need him.

But what about his son? Would Schyler be happier raised as a Langworthy?

Would he be better off without Night in his life?

COLLEEN WELLESLEY had called upon all the branches of the Confidential organization for help. The operatives had gathered for a light informal meal, then followed Colleen to the hidden meeting room in the basement of the Royal Flush.

The Confidential organization, which had begun as a division of the Department of Public Safety, had started in Texas, then expanded to Montana and Chicago. Colleen had been there before she had taken over the new Colorado branch. Mitchell Forbes, Jake Cantrell and his wife Abby came from

Texas. Vincent Romeo had arrived with Law Davies from Chicago. And Frank Connolly showed up with his brilliant scientist wife, C.J., from Montana.

"Sorry Whitney couldn't make it," Vincent said. "But she's pregnant."

"Understandable." Colleen smiled and gestured for everyone to take a seat, then began without preamble. "I've asked you all here because of our concern over the ramifications of research and biological warfare." She passed out folders, a photo of Teddy Grace included in each packet.

"In the early '60s, Dr. Theodore Grace graduated at the top of his class at Yale with a Ph.D. in microbiology. He was recruited to work at the federal government's biological weapons research center, Fort Detrick, in Frederick, MD. He became one of their leading scientists, and made breakthrough discoveries in how to incubate and disperse doses of microbes that could infect millions of people. He was working on highly promising experiments in combining viral and bacterial DNA when President Nixon shut down bio weapons research in 1969. Grace became bitter and frustrated and went to a private company, but was even more frustrated with the restrictions. So, he began experimenting in his basement."

Colleen sighed. "Recently, we've learned that he has not only resurfaced, but that he has been conducting germ warfare on the unsuspecting public." She indicated the second page in the file, a copy of the CDC's report explaining the test results on Q fever and the germ testing Grace had conducted on Holly and the Langworthy baby.

A series of concerned noises rippled through the room. Colleen filled them in on the details they'd uncovered concerning the Silver Rapids flu and the Langworthy baby kidnapping.

"I'm asking for your help in exploring this problem. As of now, we have lost contact with our operative, Night Walker. Walker went in three days ago to track down Grace's laboratory, which we believe is somewhere between Ouray and Gunnison." She pointed to a map of Colorado on the wall, pinpoints marking the general area where they believed the laboratory was located. "In the surveillance room, we've linked to the files at the DPS office, DMV and FBI, but still haven't determined the exact location of Grace's lab, although Walker called in coordinates which we're trying to verify."

C.J. spoke up. "I'll look at any medical reports you have on the bug that caused the Silver Rapids flu and get back to you on the possible results. But judging from first sight, since two people have died already, if Grace unleashes the germ in a larger or more lethal dosage, such as a mushroom cloud, the result could be devastating."

The agents murmured agreement.

"If he's as crazy as you say, he may already have plans in motion for widespread testing of other bacteria," C.J. said. "You need to find him as soon as possible. This type of thing would be much more deadly than the anthrax scare."

"Exactly what we're trying to prevent," Colleen said. "We don't know what other kinds of germs he's working on. He may have nerve gases, as well as other deadly germ strains."

"We'll find him," Vincent said. "And get rid of the problem."

Colleen held up a warning hand. "We want Grace alive. Vincent, you and Frank will go in and follow Night's trail. Jake and Abby, you're excellent at getting into tight places, you go with them to investigate Grace's lab." She gestured toward Lawson Davies. "And Law, we'll need you for legal advice once we capture Grace."

"With all that's going on in the Middle East and our concerns for defensive measures against the possibility of chemical warfare, Grace might prove invaluable," C.J. said.

"Right." Colleen frowned. "Once we have him, we'll turn him over to the government. They'll take it from there." She stood. "But first things first. Let's see if we can find Grace's laboratory. After we rescue Holly Langworthy and her baby, we'll try to save the rest of the world from Grace's insanity."

LIFE WAS too short to settle. He had been settling all his life.

Putting all his hopes and dreams into the hands of others, then watching as they fell apart, ripped away by lies and conniving wealthy people who turned their personal crisis into a widespread public cry.

The Langworthys.

He hated them all.

Celia Langworthy, Samuel, Holly. They all had to pay.

He tacked the pictures he'd cut from the newspaper onto the bulletin board in his private office, shoving stick pins into the heads of each of the family members who had been photographed nonstop for the past four months. They had ruined his life.

And after he'd played their games. Suffering through the election that should have named him governor. Suffering through the humiliation of watching another Langworthy rise to the public's attention.

And all because of that damn baby.

He'd tried to get rid of it. Hoped they never found it. That that crazy scientist had hidden it away for good.

And Holly…when the time was right, and he got his hands on her, she'd wish she'd never given birth to that child. The child that had created so much sympathy for Joshua Langworthy that the public had voted him in as their leader.

When all along it should have been him.

NIGHT HAD just let himself doze off on the floor beside the crib when the sound of the door being unlocked jarred him. He froze, acclimating to the darkness and honing in on his instinct that something wasn't right. Why would Grace return in the middle of the night, unless he meant to harm him or Holly?

He rolled to an attack position, and slid behind the back of the door to prepare for a surprise move when Mary stepped into the room. He saw the shadow of a gun, the weapon trembling in her hand as she peered around the room. Then she spotted Holly asleep on the cot and visibly relaxed. She obviously assumed he was asleep in the room with her.

He held his breath. Waited in the shadows to see what she planned to do, watching as she approached the crib.

Realization dawned when he noticed the diaper bag thrown over her shoulder. She was going to snatch Schyler.

She stopped by the crib, and he padded up behind her. ''What will your boss say when he discovers your intentions?''

She whirled around, wide-eyed with her own brand of craziness and swung the pistol at him. He knocked her arm upward and she cried out. Then he grabbed her hand and tried to disarm her, but the gun dislodged and fired into the ceiling. She screamed, the bullet ricocheted from the cavernous ceiling to the floor. Another shot fired, barely missing his foot as he jerked the gun from her. Holly bolted up and ran toward the crib. Sky's piercing cry rent the air. Bertram raced in.

Night pivoted to aim the gun at Bertram, but Bertram raised his own weapon. Then suddenly Holly jumped Mary from the back. Mary fought like a wildcat. Holly gripped her around the neck, trying to bring the woman down, but when Mary elbowed her in the ribs, Holly lost her grip and fell backward. Her head hit the concrete wall beside him with a loud whack. His heart stopped.

Holly sank to the floor in a lifeless pool, a stream of blood forming a puddle as it trickled from her head.

Chapter Six

Seconds later, Grace ran in, looking haggard and bug-eyed. "What the hell is going on?"

Night glanced at Holly, willing her to be all right, while keeping his gaze on Bertram's gun. Mary had huddled in the corner with the baby, her movements jerky with desperation as she tried to soothe Schyler.

"Your nurse was trying to kidnap my son," Night said.

"Is that true?" Grace roared.

Bertram nodded in affirmation and Grace ran a hand through his white hair, sending it spiraling out wildly. "Good god, Bertram, I told you to keep an eye on her. She's a loose cannon."

"He's my baby now," Mary said in a singsongy voice that sounded as if she'd lost touch with reality. "My baby, my baby, my baby…"

Holly moaned and Grace knelt beside her, then pushed her hair back from her forehead to check the gash. Night gritted his teeth, wanting to go to her. But he needed to let the situation settle before Bertram lost his cool and took a shot at him or Holly.

"She needs stitches," Grace snapped.

Holly stirred, and Night considered trying to wrestle the gun from Bertram, but Holly was in no condition to travel.

And he would not leave the fortress without her and his son.

"Help me get her to one of the labs, and I'll stitch her up," Grace said.

Bertram frowned. "Shall we tie him up first?"

"Let me carry her," Night said, not trusting that the crazed scientist wouldn't inject her with some other virus.

Grace nodded reluctantly. "Lock Mary inside with the child. When we get these two taken care of, you come back and get her under control. I haven't made it this far to have some overly emotional nurse screw up my plans." He shot Mary a menacing look, but she was lost in her own world, humming and talking gibberish to Schyler. The baby seemed to sense that things weren't right. His wailing escalated several decibels.

Night leaned down, gently easing Holly into his arms. She cried out and tried to fight him, but he whispered her name. "Shh, it's okay. I have you."

She opened her eyes slightly, wincing with pain, and he gazed into her eyes, silently telling her to hang on.

"Schyler?"

The fear in her voice wrenched his emotions. How had he ever thought she might not care about their child? "He's okay, Holly. Don't worry. Schyler's fine."

Although judging from Mary's bizarre behavior, he hated to leave his son in her hands for a minute.

And he certainly didn't trust that she might not try to escape with him again.

HOLLY WAS barely cognizant of being carried from the room and placed on a gurney, but the sound of her son's cries stabbed at the pain slicing through her head. She wanted to be with him, to hold him, to take him home where he belonged.

A needle jabbed at her forehead and she winced. She remembered the first day Grace had brought her here, the faint sense that he was drugging her. But why?

Then the strong odor of antiseptic assaulted her, and she felt numb. The skin on her forehead tingled, and she tried to keep her eyes open, but she was so tired she couldn't move. The room was spinning. Sweat beaded on her upper lip and trickled down her chin. She was cold. So cold her teeth chattered.

What had happened to her? Where was she now? What was Grace doing to her? Had he infected her with another germ or virus?

Then Night's voice. "You're okay, Holly. You have a concussion. Grace is stitching the gash on your head."

That explained the throbbing pain in her skull, the reason the light hurt her eyes and she couldn't keep them open. She relented to the darkness again and prayed Night would protect their son.

But fear seeped in. The other shots...she was sure Grace had injected her with something else. Had he given her another one of his experimental germ tests? Was she going to die before they could rescue their baby?

NIGHT PACED back and forth across the small dank room where Grace had locked him and Holly, sneaking glimpses of her constantly to make certain she was still breathing. Frustration knotted his stomach. They were back to square one.

He searched his brain for a plan of escape, a way to trick Bertram and Grace, but Holly's injury temporarily handicapped them. He could carry the baby across the terrain they'd need to cover, but carrying Holly and Schyler and making a speedy exit would be damn near impossible.

He slammed his fist against the concrete wall, welcoming the physical pain as blood trickled from the scratches on his knuckles. He had never felt so powerless and helpless in his life. Not even as a child when he had been shunned at school, when some of the richer white kids had called him names. When they had laughed and made fun of his father's dark skin and the strange ways of the Cheyenne. And then life on the reservation where he and his mother had tried to fit in…

Holly moaned, and he fought the urge to go to her and comfort her. He could not allow himself to care about her. To touch her.

"Don't go, Night…"

He jerked his head around. She twisted her head back and forth as if she were dreaming, having a nightmare. Except their nightmare was real.

"Please, find Schyler…please." Her soft cries continued, her pleas to have her son back destroying the walls he'd erected to keep his feelings at bay.

"Schyler." Tears rolled down her face, the ugly purple bruising and swelling above her eye reminding him that she had been hurt trying to save their son. "Don't take my baby away. Please... No!"

Unable to stand her agony any longer, he told himself he was simply offering comfort as he would do to any person under his protective custody. Any client.

"I want my son..." her voice broke, and he stretched out on the cot beside her, and pulled her into his arms.

"Shh, Holly. We're here now, Schyler's in the other room." He continued to murmur soft words of encouragement while he stroked her hair and rocked her in his arms. "As soon as you're feeling better, we'll get Sky and leave."

She snuggled up to him, curled one hand on his chest, and groaned, then finally drifted into a more peaceful sleep. Her hair tickled his chin, and her breath bathed his neck, but he steeled himself against his feelings.

He had not slept in days himself though, and realized he should rest while he could. He might need extra energy to carry Holly when they made a run for it.

So, he closed his eyes, trying hard not to inhale Holly's sultry scent or allow himself to enjoy the feel of her curves melting into the hard planes of his body. Yet memories returned to haunt him.

The flirty smiles she'd sneaked him when he'd first accepted the security job at the Langworthy mansion. The instantaneous reaction his body had at the sight of her. The way he'd lain in bed every night on that job, his body rock hard and throbbing, his mind drifting to impossible fantasies about the two of them together. The rich, young, beautiful college graduate, so full of life and optimism, so untainted by the dark world that held him hostage.

The image of her dressed in that evening dress the night of the party at her father's. The creamy mounds of her breasts spilling over the top of her gown. The allure of her perfume. The realization that out of all the men at the party, she had watched him throughout the evening. Telling him with those laughing green eyes that she wanted him to kiss her. Night Walker, the Native who wasn't good enough to be anything but her bodyguard. She'd wanted him in her bed.

Then he'd lost his resistance.

He welcomed the tormenting memories, letting them wash away the pain. The whisper of her kiss on his bare chest when he'd finally given in. The soft, supple way she'd opened to him, offering her innocence. The passionate way she'd clung to him while he'd pumped himself inside her. The hunger he felt every time he looked at her.

The desire that would only get him hurt and interfere with his job.

Ignoring the ache in his body, he closed his eyes, but he couldn't sleep. Instead he reviewed the details of the case as he had every night over the past few months. Images of the newspaper photos of Holly with Carlton Sanders flashed in his head. The society couple, the man everyone thought might be named assistant to the governor when Joshua Langworthy won the election. But Sanders had not been named Joshua's assistant, he had taken another position. And he'd disappeared from the limelight since the kidnapping, probably as a favor to Langworthy since the press hadn't been kind to Holly.

They'd suggested that she'd been cavorting around town, screwing Sanders while someone sneaked into the night and stole her child. Then rumors had started—they'd written that she'd been drinking, that she'd taken a sedative before she retired for the night so her illegitimate baby wouldn't disturb her beauty sleep.

Of course, Holly had avoided the media during the entire ordeal, had not even responded to the accusations about the sedative and her incompetence at motherhood. One reporter had quoted that her first words when she'd discovered her baby were, "It's all my fault," she cried.

The press had jumped on the bandwagon with that statement, offering all types of scenarios, all of which she had yet to publicly deny.

He couldn't rectify the accusations with the Holly he'd seen the past few days, the Holly who had appeared to be devastated over the loss of their child. The Holly who'd gone off on her own to the Langworthy cabin to meet the kidnapper, the one who'd attacked Mary tonight.

Still, several details about the kidnapping disturbed him, questions that had led the police to believe that someone inside the family had been involved in the kidnapping. Mainly, how had Grace or whoever had helped him gotten into the Langworthy mansion and abducted the baby from the house without being detected? The Langworthy security was state of the art. Who exactly had been in the house? Had Grace had a conspirator whom the

Langworthys trusted, someone they hadn't questioned or wouldn't suspect? The maid? A friend? Someone on Langworthy's political campaign? So far, Colorado Confidential had uncovered nothing.

Night saw Carlton Sanders's face again. Sanders had been questioned during the preliminary interviews. But what was his relationship with Holly now? Once she returned with Sky, would she and Sanders pick up where they left off?

The idea caused his body to clench with anxiety. He forced himself to another plane, a level where he separated body and mind, using the ancient skills of his ancestors as he practiced the art of mastering his control and emotions. Then, and only then, did he finally allow himself to fall asleep.

But in the wee hours of the morning, Holly's troubled cries woke him again. He lay in the darkness, holding her tightly.

"No, Daddy…no, I can't do that. I can't marry him," Holly whispered in a tortured voice. "Night doesn't know about the baby, his son…"

Jesus. She was talking about him.

"I won't, I don't want to get married. I…I don't love him." She cried out, pulling away from him as if recoiling in horror. "I could never love him, and I…won't trap him into marriage."

Night rolled to a sitting position and bolted from the bed, his heart hammering. He had known a rich princess like Holly Langworthy couldn't love a man like himself, a man torn between a world of ancient customs and modern evil.

But hearing her say the words aloud cut him to the core.

WHEN HOLLY WOKE, she realized three things. Her head was killing her, she had had nightmares of her father trying to coerce her into marrying Carlton Sanders and she felt very much alone. Where was Night?

Had Grace come for him, taken him away? Killed him?

Panic rippled through her. She tried to sit up, but a dizzy spell caught her off guard and she swayed. Bracing herself with one hand, she lay back and waited until it passed, then rolled to her side to check the room.

Night stood with his back to her, his massive shoulders squared, his body so rigid she ached to touch him and soothe away the tension. But he didn't want her.

Hadn't he told her that enough times?

Although he had joined her in bed for a while. She'd felt the warmth of his body and heard his low gruff voice reassuring her. But maybe she'd been dreaming then, too.

''Night?''

If possible, he stiffened even more, then pivoted toward her, the gentle assurance that he had offered her the day before vacant from his cold brown eyes. He seemed so distant, a million miles away.

''Did something happen?'' Nausea rolled through her. She remembered the fight, Mary trying to take her baby, Bertram running in with the gun, then pain and needles and fear.

He stared at her, his mouth in a flat line, and fear pounced in her veins.

"Is Schyler okay? Mary didn't escape with him, did she?"

"No."

She eased herself up, fighting queasiness, giving her eyes time to adjust to the dimness of the room and to let the blurriness recede.

"How do you feel?"

She raised a hand to touch the bandage on her forehead. "I'll live."

He nodded curtly. "But not up to traveling?"

She took a deep breath. Had Grace given her some virus? She felt strange, disoriented, hot and cold at the same time. But she would not complain to Night. She didn't have time to be weak. "If you can sneak us out of here with Schyler, I'll do my best to keep up."

He almost smiled, then seemed to catch himself. "Then I have a plan." He came over and sat down beside her on the bed. She started to reach out and touch him, but he stiffened and spread his hands on his thighs, so she clutched the blanket covering her.

Wearing that iron mask expression of his, he leaned over and mouthed, "The place might be bugged. Now listen, this is what I want you to do...."

THE RATIONAL part of Night's mind warned him Holly wasn't ready to try an escape, but he refused to listen. Every minute they spent in Grace's clutches made them vulnerable.

Just as every minute he spent with Holly made him vulnerable.

An emotion he could not afford to feel. He had

a job to do and he needed to focus. Not only did his son's life depend on it, but it was imperative that Colorado Confidential stop Grace's chemical warfare research. The only way they could determine his exact activities was to seize control of Grace and his lab. Night had to escape, contact his fellow operatives, let the DPS know what they were dealing with, so they could confiscate all of Grace's files.

Who knew when Grace might completely lose his mind and decide to attack another segment of the population with one of his dangerous germs? Or what if Grace sold some of his germs or a virus to a foreign government, one of the enemy countries who would use Grace's work to destroy the U.S.?

With either scenario, they'd have a national crisis on their hands, if not an international one.

Night tried to distance himself from the fear in Holly's eyes. He couldn't forget the words she'd murmured in her dreams—she didn't love him. She would never marry him.

"Are you ready?"

She nodded, then stretched back out on the bed, preparing herself to play the role they'd discussed. He banged on the door. "Grace, come here! Holly needs some pain medication! Can you hear me?"

It took several minutes and more yelling before he heard footsteps. Thankfully, Grace appeared instead of Bertram. His eyes looked sluggish, his hair disheveled as if he'd been running his hands through it, and his glasses sat crookedly on the end of his nose.

"I brought some Demerol." He produced the needle, then closed the door and approached Holly.

She played the part well, thrashing her head back and forth, holding her temples with her fingers and groaning. "Make it stop, my head's going to explode, please…"

Grace patted her arm, a frown puckering his bushy eyebrows as he felt her forehead. "Oh, my, you feel a little warm." He tapped the hypodermic. "This should make your head feel better and let you sleep. I'll come back to take more blood and figure out what's going on."

Just as Grace raised the needle, Night jumped him from behind. Grace was agile for an old man, but adrenaline surged through Night. He landed a swift blow to Grace's midsection, knocked the shot from his hand, and karate chopped him at the base of his neck, sending the man to the floor. Then he grabbed the needle and jammed it into Grace's arm, bent and searched his pocket for the man's gun. When he found it, he aimed it, ready to fire.

Holly jumped off the bed, leaped over Grace's body and they raced into the hallway.

Chapter Seven

Holly held her breath as they darted through the corridors. Soon they would get Sky, soon they would escape. Soon they would be home.

She had to believe that.

Her head was swimming, but she clutched Night's hand to steady herself, and crept behind him as he rounded the corner to the corridor housing the nursery. She was amazed at the ease with which he found his way through the maze of hallways, how his senses guided him. He moved so silently she couldn't even hear his boots on the hard flooring beneath them.

How long would Grace stay unconscious? Had he already awakened and alerted Bertram they were on their way? What would Grace do to them if he caught them?

Her chest heaved as Night slowed, crooking his thumb toward the nursery and gesturing for her to stay behind him. Sky's cries echoed through the closed doorway, tugging at her heart. Night had taken the keys from Grace before they'd run. He jammed the key in the hole and slowly turned the knob. Motioning for her to hide behind him, he raised the gun, then slid into the room. Holly inched up behind him. Mary was bent over the changing table, cooing to Schyler in an attempt to calm his cries.

Expecting Bertram or Dr. Grace, Mary's eyes widened in alarm when she saw Night wielding a gun.

Mary hurriedly gathered the baby to her chest. "You can't have him, he's my baby now."

Holly bit her tongue to keep from lashing out. Any noise might alert Bertram.

"Just stay still and you won't get hurt," Night warned.

Mary's expression turned desperate. "No, you can't have him."

But Night stalked toward her, his size overpowering hers as he reached for Schyler. Mary tightened her grip, but Holly hurried forward and took the baby. Schyler quieted instantly.

"Sit down in the chair," Night instructed.

When Mary remained frozen, Night pushed her into it, tied a cloth around her mouth, then grabbed her arms and tied them behind her to the rocking chair. At the same time, Holly stuffed some bottles and diapers in the diaper bag, then reached for the toy bunny. "Get that blanket," Night instructed. "And a hat and extra blanket for the baby."

Holly obeyed, then they ran out the door, locking Mary in behind them.

Night checked every corner, searching for Dr. Grace or Bertram. Once he heard footsteps and shoved Holly into the shadow of an overhang. They

waited until the sound passed, then he waved for
her to follow. Instead of going toward the door he'd
entered near the waterfall, Night went the opposite
direction down a long, winding hallway. Holly realized he wanted to locate the helicopter, but wondered if they were wasting time.

His instincts seemed to be on target though, as
only minutes later, after winding in and out of several corridors housing labs, they found a door that
led upstairs to a garage area which could have held
a chopper.

"Damn it, it's empty." Night guided her outside.
"Bertram must be on an errand for Grace." Night
assumed Bertram was the pilot.

Holly nodded, breathing in fresh air and light for
the first time in days as they stepped outside. Night
guided her to a patch of woods behind the side entrance to the fortress, and placed Sky in her arms
while he quickly dug his backpack out of the underbrush.

Suddenly Grace appeared, staggering from the
drug, but waving another gun. He aimed and fired
at Night.

Night shoved Holly forward. "Run!"

She darted into the woods, hugging her son to her
as she jumped over roots and bushes. Night followed, dodging a bullet. Their only hope was that
Grace was too weak from the injection to keep chasing after them.

WHEN THEY finally reached a small ravine and
Night decided they had cleared the gunfire, he
stopped long enough to fashion a baby carrier out

of the blanket. Then Holly helped him secure Schyler to his back. Holly was winded and flushed, but she hadn't complained. Undaunted, she slung the backpack over her shoulder as if she tackled hiking the rocky terrain of the Colorado mountains every day.

"We're heading southwest toward Ouray." He pointed through the thicket of trees to the steep jagged peaks beyond. "I parked the jeep in a ravine at the base of that mountain."

"How far?"

"Two days." Unfortunately Grace had confiscated Night's cell phone. "I have another phone back in the jeep, we can call for help. Colleen and the others must have gotten lost in the storm."

Holly nodded. "You think Grace followed us?"

"I don't know. He probably contacted Bertram in the chopper. Be on the alert."

She nodded again, her concerned gaze on Schyler, who wiggled behind Night, cooing.

"We're taking you home," Holly whispered. "Where that crazy Dr. Grace will never get to you again."

Night tensed, wondering if she would shut him out of her son's life as well. But they'd have to discuss their relationship later. "Let's go. We need to travel while it's daylight. Once the sun goes down, the temperature will drop."

Winter sunshine slashed through the pines and fur trees, splicing shades of color over the pearly white snow and icy ridges as they climbed. Since the lab had been built in a small canyon, literally carved out of the San Juan Mountains, they had to climb over the mountain, then descend on the other side. In November the daytime temperature ranged in the thirties, but at night dipped into the low teens, sometimes lower. Night intended to get them to shelter before then.

The elements could be brutal at high altitudes, and exhaustion would make Holly and the baby more susceptible to injury or illness. A light snowstorm had already struck, but dark storm clouds hovered in the distance, promising heavier snowfall before night.

Not wanting to alarm Holly, he kept his worries to himself, and maintained a steady pace, guiding them toward the general location of Ouray and the ravine where he'd left the jeep, although he had to zigzag around the mountain to avoid some of the more difficult impasses.

The San Juan Mountains were rugged, sharp inclines with gorges that made many patches nearly impossible to climb, especially for an amateur or a couple with a baby. So far, Schyler had been amicable, cooing and jabbering, and later, dozing off. Holly remained quiet, climbing behind him, matching his pace, only occasionally reaching for him to take her hand and help her cross the narrow ledges. Those moments were awkward, the tension between them palpable, especially since he couldn't shake the words she'd muttered in her sleep.

I don't love him, I could never love him.

Hadn't Charity said the same thing? *I only went to bed with him, Mother, I'd never marry a Native.*

He rubbed the name bead necklace. Holly's

words stung even more because they had created a child together.

A rumbling sound broke through his thoughts and he raised his hand to shield the sun from his eyes, searching the skies. Colleen would most likely send a search party in a chopper, too.

But Grace had probably alerted Bertram and they would be combing the area for them.

He spotted a semblance of a trail and turned right, veering onto a faint footpath that tunneled between rows and rows of dark-limbed pines. Better to be hidden by the forest than out in the open where Bertram could spot them if he flew overhead. Unfortunately, the shade of the trees robbed the air of the sun's warmth, and as he checked over his shoulder, he saw Holly blow out a stream of foggy breath. Nestled inside the makeshift blanket baby carrier with his cap on, Schyler still slept, safe and warm for now.

Holly glanced up then and met his gaze. Her cheeks were rosy from the exertion, her nose slightly red, her eyes bright with the earnestness of their hike. She latched onto a tree limb to support herself as she trekked up the incline.

A brief glimpse of hunger flared in her eyes. Or had he imagined it?

No, it flickered again, the same kind of yearning that she'd worn like an open invitation when he'd played bodyguard at her house. The kind of naked longing that made him want to forget their different lifestyles, their backgrounds, the fact that she'd given birth to his son without bothering to inform him.

Dammit. After hearing her say she didn't love him, how could he possibly still want her?

BY EARLY EVENING, snow was falling in a thick fog, and Holly had lost track of the hours and which direction they were traveling. Night led them through the darkest parts of the forest-covered mountain, zigzagging around various gorges and cliffs, siding around the ridges and bypassing the more straightforward open areas. She understood. He didn't want Bertram to spot them. She'd heard the helicopter twice, circling above, searching for them as a hunter stalks his prey. But the climbing was hard, especially since she still felt weak from the concussion.

Night had no problem. His physical prowess and strength astounded her, as did his calm demeanor. She'd never seen anyone so instinctively in tune with his surroundings. It was as if he and nature had become one, as if he only had to listen and the wind or the sun told him the right direction to go. Had he inherited those instincts from his Cheyenne ancestors? Had her son?

Her father didn't want Schyler to know any part of his Native American heritage. But could she deny her son the strong bond of fatherhood? Especially now that she knew Night wanted to be a part of his life?

And what had happened back at the lab? One minute, she'd thought she and Night were bridging the gap between them. But since she'd hit her head, he'd become more distant and brooding than before.

The smell of a dead animal penetrated the sharp

piney smell of the woods, and she glanced to her right, down the jutting cliff and grimaced. A small deer lay on its side, the stark rawness of its bloody carcass reminding her of their peril. She dragged her gaze away, focusing on Night's broad back. He climbed on with amazing skill and fortitude, not winded, his body resilient and full of energy while hers sagged with fatigue.

She was losing steam fast. They had stopped only once, no longer than ten minutes, long enough to feed Schyler a bottle, check his diaper and grab a snack and some water from the backpack of supplies Night had packed. Night had made efforts to cover their tracks. The temperature had already begun to drop, sending a chill through her denim shirt. She desperately wished she'd had time to retrieve her coat and gloves before they'd hit the woods.

Night said nothing to her as he led the way, although he constantly spoke in hushed tones to their son, telling him about the earth, naming the trees, describing tracking methods and assuring him they would soon rest. If she hadn't been so exhausted herself, his brooding manner and intentional dismissal of her presence might have grated on her nerves. But her feet ached so badly she thought she couldn't move them anymore. Blisters rubbed raw beneath her boots, her hands were numb and stiff, and in spite of the fact that she was shivering from the cold, a hot flush beaded her face every few minutes and chased down her spine.

She had a fever, felt as if she was coming down with a flu. But even if she was sick, she would damn well not complain or even mention it to Night. Night had risked his life to rescue her and their son, and she would not slow him down or solidify his opinion of her as a pampered rich, weak girl. Besides, if they stopped, Grace might catch them and take Schyler. She'd die before she'd let him get his hands on her son again.

Another step. Another. One foot in front of the next. She could do this.

By the time they crested the smaller peak, the sun was already falling, the snowfall thickening in intensity. At a tall hickory tree, he hesitated to study the area.

"There's an old mine shaft and a cave just north of here. If we can make it there, we'll settle in for the night."

"You don't want to continue on?"

His dark eyes raked over her. "I could, but you look like you need to rest. Besides, it would be too cold to chance keeping Schyler outside all night."

She nodded. "Of course. I just don't want to be the hold up."

He offered her a small smile. "You've done well."

Tears pressed against her eyelids at his compliment. She was trying so hard. But her feet and legs cramped, and a dull throbbing had taken root deep inside her bones. She felt like she might collapse any second.

"Take five minutes. Get a drink of water." He gestured toward a stump, and Holly dropped onto it. Schyler flapped his hands around as if waving. "Bababbab…"

''You are the best baby.'' Holly smiled and reached out to shake his fingers.

Night shifted the baby in the pack so that she could take him out. ''I'll be right back.''

Panic slammed into her. ''Where are you going?''

He cocked a brow, and a small grin flickered upward. She realized his intentions and could have kicked herself for panicking. She should take the moment to relieve herself, too, only she must be dehydrated because she didn't feel the need.

''Get some water, Holly. And give Schyler a bottle. We're at high altitude. Don't forget to hydrate yourself and him.''

She forced herself to sip from the canteen, then gave Schyler some formula, although her teeth were chattering. Night returned within a couple of minutes, his expression a mask.

''How are your feet holding up?''

She bit down on her lip. ''Fine.''

''Blisters?''

''Yes.'' How had he known?

He knelt beside her and gently removed her boot while she bounced a squirming Schyler up and down, blowing kisses on his belly.

Night winced as he examined her red, blistered ankles and toes. ''You should have said something.''

She shrugged. ''A few blisters are nothing if it means saving our baby's life.''

He dug inside the backpack, produced some gauze and cream, then slowly applied it to the tender places. Holly stiffened at his touch, then relaxed as he smeared on the ointment. It felt so nice to have him touching her again, to have his warmth replace the chill that had invaded her. He didn't look up once though, almost as if he didn't want to admit the intimacy of the act, although she thought she'd detected a slight flinch in his eyes.

"Thank you, Night," Holly said softly.

His hand stilled, then his gaze slid up to meet hers. Instead of acknowledging her though, he pressed his mouth into a tight line, then stood and took the baby. "Put on your shoes and let's get going. The sun's going down, it'll get cold fast."

She did as he instructed, biting her lip so she wouldn't cry out as she tugged the shoes back onto her feet. When she tried to stand, she swayed slightly. Maybe she was getting altitude sickness. She had never experienced it before, but...that thought was much preferable than wondering what germ or virus Grace might have injected in her system. If it was something deadly...

"Walk on your toes," Night instructed, "it takes the pressure off the balls of your feet."

She steadied herself. "Is that an old Cheyenne trick?"

He didn't smile. "Yes. My ancestors used to travel many miles a day for food, hunting for buffalo, searching for new places to live when the white man ran them off."

Without another word Holly helped place Schyler on Night's back, and they began hiking around the mountain again. Holly sighed. Would it always be this way between them? Would their worlds always divide them?

How would their son ever fit in between the two

worlds if she and Night couldn't forge some kind of relationship between the two of them?

NIGHT REFUSED to admit that simply touching Holly's bare feet had made him feel connected to her, that he'd wanted to do more than offer bandages and ointment to assuage her discomfort. Fatigue strained her posture, the dark circles beneath her eyes and the graying pallor of her skin indicating she was still weak from the concussion. Her breathing had become progressively more labored over the hours.

He regretted pushing her so hard, but moved on relentlessly. He had no choice. As darkness descended and they traveled through some of the most isolated, steepest parts of the mountain, she cursed beneath her breath. If she thought he was a bastard, all the better. At least then he wouldn't have to endure those hungry looks she'd given him earlier.

Why did she keep looking at him with need-filled eyes if she couldn't love him?

He had always sensed the pain and suffering of an animal, especially the horses he trained, the reason some called him a horse whisperer. But he had never felt this strange connection with a person before. Especially a woman.

He didn't like it. He cherished his independence and did not want to lose himself in a female who would rip his heart out again.

He sensed the depth of Holly's fear as well as her trust, which was oddly humbling. She believed he would get them out of this danger safely. He could not let her or their son down. But neither could he forget the wide chasm between them.

He spoke to Schyler in a low voice, not wanting to alert anyone in case Grace or Bertram were closing in on their trail. What if Grace had outside sources working for him? He could have called in help to track them down.

"These are cypress trees," he said, pointing out the shape of their leaves to Schyler. "And look at this marking, this is where a cougar has sharpened his claws on the tree trunk. These trees mean we might be close to water, son." He continued talking, describing the vegetation, explaining to his son how to tell directions by the sun and pausing occasionally to listen to the forest sounds, naming those as well. Schyler cooed and babbled as if he understood.

Night was certain he did. He was part Cheyenne, these things would come naturally. Holly seemed to be slowing down quite a bit. Her breath hissed through the darkness as they approached the last of the small hills near the cave and the old mines. If he remembered correctly, a stream ran through the mountain at that point, too. It would be an excellent place to stop and eat, and seek cover for the night.

An owl hooted in the distance. The lone cry of a prairie wolf cut through the inky night. He picked up his pace, willing Holly to do the same, pushing harder and harder, climbing through thick underbrush that clawed at his legs and arms. Just as he crested the top of the hill, he glanced over his shoulder, but he didn't see Holly. Damn.

He froze and listened, tuning in to the sounds of the forest. She would break through the brush behind him any second. But all was quiet. Eerily still. He stared at the bushes again, waiting several more seconds, his pulse accelerating. When she still didn't appear, fear pounded in his chest.

He ran back down the incline, shoving his way through the brush, panting as he broke through. About ten feet down the slope, he spotted her. She was sprawled facedown in the icy snow.

And she wasn't moving.

HE WAS ON TO them now. With every mile he crossed, he was moving closer. So close he could smell the sweet bliss of revenge at his fingertips.

He stared at the latest newspaper article chronicling the kidnapping and grimaced. Ironic, the one thing that should have torn the Langworthys apart, the missing illegitimate child, had played in Joshua's favor. *He* should have been governor, head of the state, getting the accolades and glittery shine of the press, not smooth-talking Joshua. He hadn't sacrificed and stuck his neck out only to be caught. And if Teddy Grace was captured, he might squeal.

That would ruin *his* career. And he had big plans.

Damn Joshua for getting engaged and ruining those plans. If there was anything the voters responded to more than the sympathy card, it was the idealistic romanticism of an impending wedding. Now Joshua's face had become a household name in the state of Colorado.

The chopper engine suddenly coughed and spat, the blizzard conditions making it bounce above the storm clouds. He'd have to bring it down here in the damn wilderness, then go in on foot and finish

Get FREE BOOKS and a FREE GIFT when you play the...

LAS VEGAS GAME

*Just scratch off
the gold box with a coin.
Then check below to see
the gifts you get!*

YES!
I have scratched off the gold Box. Please send me my **2 FREE BOOKS** and **gift for which I qualify.** I understand that I am under no obligation to purchase any books as explained on the back of this card.

382 HDL DVCG   **182 HDL DVCM**

FIRST NAME	LAST NAME

ADDRESS

APT.#	CITY

STATE/PROV.	ZIP/POSTAL CODE

(H-IA-12/03)

7	7	7	Worth TWO FREE BOOKS plus a BONUS Mystery Gift!
🍒	🍒	🍒	Worth TWO FREE BOOKS!
🔔	🔔	♣	TRY AGAIN!

Offer limited to one per household and not valid to current Harlequin Intrigue® subscribers. All orders subject to approval.

the job. But leaving the chopper would give him an escape later. And no one would be the wiser. The Langworthys didn't even know he could fly. They would never suspect him. His pulse raced with excitement at the thought of revenge.

Yes, soon Holly Langworthy would die. And then Samuel Langworthy would be sorry for all he had done.

Chapter Eight

As if Schyler sensed Night's anxiety, he began to whimper. Night automatically shifted into the cadence of his Cheyenne brothers, the tone he used to quiet the animals. "Shh, my son, I'm certain your mother is going to be fine. She's probably just exhausted from the day and that concussion."

Night knelt and gently brushed Holly's tangled hair from her face, grimacing at the sight of her pale skin. Snowflakes dotted her cheeks as well as perspiration. Icy crystals clung to her auburn eyelashes and hair. Her thin denim shirt and jeans were soaked, her hands red and dry.

But at least she was breathing.

He laid a hand on her cheek to try to wake her. She was burning up with fever. "Good God, Holly, why didn't you say something?" Had Grace infected her with another germ before he'd arrived?

Schyler whimpered again, and Night murmured softly to console him while he reached inside the backpack, grabbed a water bottle, and turned Holly over in his arms. He cradled her head and urged her to drink. She was shaking uncontrollably. "Come on, sweetheart, take a sip. You have to get some fluids in your system to combat the fever.''

She moaned and shifted her head back and forth, cupping her head in her hands as if it hurt. What other symptoms did she have? Had she been suffering all day and not told him?

Not like you gave her much of a chance. You shut her out, pushed her to this....

''Holly, did Grace give you something?''

She groaned.

''Tell me, honey. You're feverish, did he give you anything?''

''Shots,'' she choked out. ''Don't know what...''

He forced a sip of water down her throat, dried the slow trickle that dribbled down her cheek with the back of his hand, then closed the canteen, panic gnawing at him. ''We'll have to carry your mama for a while,'' he told Schyler. ''Hang on, son.''

Gathering Holly into his arms, he cocooned her to him, making certain Schyler was still snug on his back. Then he stalked through the bushes and climbed the hill again, increasing his pace so he could reach the cave. He had very little with him in the way of medical supplies. Nothing for an unknown bug.

Stalking through the thick wedge of trees, he searched his mind for memories of the medicine man's magic. He would have to depend on the ways of his forefathers to lower Holly's fever. Either that or a miracle. Maybe the Confidential team would sweep in and find them.

Only, Night had purposely hiked through the invisible parts of the mountain to avoid being spotted by Bertram. Their location was well hidden by the thick forest surrounding them.

Besides, he didn't believe in miracles.

But he did believe in the spirits and the shaman's cures.

Would they be powerful enough to counteract the sophisticated strain of whatever disease Grace might have infected her with?

IT TOOK HIM almost another hour to locate the cave. By then, Schyler was irritable and his own arms strained from carrying Holly. She had barely stirred, moaning occasionally, looking paler by the minute, her teeth chattering violently. He hesitated at the mouth of the cave, listening for sounds of animals inside in case a bear or another wild animal had claimed the shelter as their winter residence.

When he heard nothing, he padded inside the entrance, allowing his night vision to scan the inside for visitors. A trickle of water inside the cave reminded him they were near a stream. Good, he could use the water to bathe Holly and heat some tea. He shuffled inside and carried her to the corner, deep enough to shield them from the elements but not so deep that they couldn't escape if trouble arrived. He removed the blanket from the backpack, spread it on the dry-packed earth, then removed the one from his back and set Schyler down beside Holly, covering them both with the blanket. Schyler patted the area, whining as he looked over at his mother with big eyes as if he wondered what had happened to the woman who'd been cooing to him this morning.

"We have to collect more wood and build a fire, then find some roots and herbs to help make your mama well."

Schyler babbled something, and Night wondered if his son was hungry. He hated to take him out into the elements again, but Holly was too weak to care for him.

Insecurity stabbed at him. *What kind of father are you? Don't you know how to take care of your son?*

"Come on, sport. I'll feed you dinner after we get that fire going." He wrapped the baby back up, covering his head and ears.

Sky whined again, and he patted his back. "I'm sorry, son. Be brave for your mama."

Although it was fairly warm inside the cave, it would get colder during the night and he needed to heat some of the herbs he planned to mix for the herbal tea. Besides, they would need the fire during the long cold night.

And if they had to stay longer.

The snow fell in thick waves as he exited the cave. The wind churned through the trees, swirling the snow to a blinding visibility. Night spent the next half hour gathering extra kindling and building the fire, explaining to Schyler each step along the way. Holly slept restlessly, twisting her head from side to side, shivering with fever. He felt her forehead again. Her temperature had spiked even higher.

"Now, we look for herbs and roots," he told Sky. "To make medicine to heal your mama."

Outside, he unearthed a hollowed-out stump from some brush, pulled it from the ground and used it to carry water. The snow was at least two feet deep now, the conditions escalating into a full-fledged blizzard. Knowing he needed to get back to Holly, he hurriedly searched the wintry trees for roots and berries, having to hunt deeper into the forest to find the ones he needed, ones he'd seen the medicine woman use in the herbal teas and pouches to heal the children at the reservation. When he finally returned to the cave, he placed the plants, roots and bark by the fire to dry them.

He dug in the backpack, fished out a jar of food and fed his son, then gave him a bottle while the water heated. Meanwhile, he took some of the roots and bark and crushed them into the log bowl, and mixed them with water to make an herbal tea. Schyler rubbed at his eyes. Night made a pallet for the baby with the baby blanket and laid him far enough away from the fire to be warm but still safe. He tucked the bunny beside Sky to comfort him. He shouldn't take any chances. What if Holly was contagious?

Schyler cooed, and Night stroked his back. "Go to sleep now, my son, so I can take care of your mama." As if their adventure today had taken its toll on Schyler, he curled onto his stomach with his rump in the air, rubbed his eyes with his fist, then clutched the stuffed bunny and soon fell asleep. Night stared at his baby a second longer, his heart clenching with love, then turned to Holly.

Night slowly pulled the blanket back from her and stripped off her soggy clothes, gritting his teeth at the way the trembling had seized her. Her pale body glowed in the soft firelight, reminding him of the night he'd made love to her. Of all the times he'd dreamed of touching her since.

He wished he was removing her clothes now to do the same. Not because he feared she might be dying.

Trying to ignore the instantaneous reaction his body had to the sight of her golden skin, he tore one of the cloth diapers from the bag into strips, then dipped it in the water to bathe Holly's face. Slowly, he let the water trickle over her, wiping and patting the tender places of her body, hoping to temper her fever, all the time murmuring words of comfort in the language of the Plains. Finally, he covered her with the blanket and applied cold compresses to her forehead. Then he forced her to drink some of the herbal tea, holding her head and coaching her to swallow.

When he'd gotten her to down nearly a whole cup, he let her rest. Memories of the ancient customs echoed through his head. The time on the reservation when he'd watched the shaman perform healing rituals. He used the crushed berries to paint his face as he'd seen his forefathers do, then turned to the fire. He chanted the songs of his people, performed the prayer ritual and dances he'd learned as a child.

"You must be one with the land and spirits," his grandmother had said. "Speak to the gods and they will hear."

He recited prayers for his son's mother in the ancient language and sang the song of his forefathers, begging the gods to save her. And when he finished the ritual and noticed she was still shivering with fever, crying softly and asking for him, he stripped off his clothes and crawled beneath the blanket. If the fire and bath hadn't warmed her, he would use his own body heat. She was his son's mother. A brave woman who had risked her life to save her child. A woman who had once given him her innocence.

He'd do anything to save her.

THE NEXT two days passed much the same, except that Schyler grew increasingly fussy. He obviously sensed something was wrong with his mother, and there were times when Night felt at a loss as to how to soothe him. The snowstorm outside dumped at least another foot of snow, the blizzard made it impossible for Night to consider moving Holly or brave the elements with a baby. Although he had wanted to be at the jeep by now, on his way back to safety with Holly and his son, waiting in the cave was the only logical thing to do under the circumstances.

Every day in the wilderness meant Bertram and Grace might find them. Hopefully, the weather had made it impossible for Bertram to fly overhead or spot them if he had. As soon as the storm let up though, Night knew the crazed scientist and his cohorts would be out looking.

Night had been gone six days now. Colorado Confidential was also looking, he was sure of it. Especially since he hadn't been able to communicate with them. But the blizzard would have slowed them down as well.

He made more herbal teas and compresses, sang the prayers and rituals daily, washing Holly and warming her at night with his body. She still hadn't woken. Every hour that she lay in misery, sweating, delirious, his fears grew. The battle between his belief in his heritage and the modern ways played war in his head. What if his medicinal efforts were useless?

She needed a hospital, medical care, a modern cure for whatever insanity Grace had inflicted upon her.

No, you must believe. Trust in the ways of your people. In your instincts.

His small son pushed himself up on his hands and knees and rocked back and forth, trying to crawl. Night stretched onto his belly on the ground in front of him, coaching, urging, smiling as Schyler struggled to move his feet and hands forward.

"Come on, my son, you can do it," he murmured. "Do it for your mama. You will have something special to show her when she wakes."

As if his son understood him, Schyler moved his right hand forward, rocked some more, then shifted his right foot, finally moving two steps before he flopped onto his belly with a squeal.

Night chuckled. "You almost have it. Another week and we'll be chasing you everywhere."

Or would they? Would Holly survive and be able to watch her son crawl? Would she see him take his first steps? And if she did, would she allow Night to be part of that picture?

Each night as he lay with her in his arms, he dreamed that the three of them were a family.

But each morning his throat was choked with the reality of the situation.

COLLEEN WELLESLEY had to check in with the operatives she'd placed in the field. "Vincent, Frank, any word on Night?"

Frank's voice echoed over the radio. "No. We tracked him partway to the Continental Divide—it looks as if he left markings. But the blizzard has made it impossible to track footprints."

"The weatherman said the storm should be moving on tonight." Colleen sighed in frustration. Samuel Langworthy had been breathing down her neck for days. He and his wife were out of their minds with worry. "Maybe tomorrow."

"Night's an expert tracker, he knows how to get through," Vincent said. "If he's found Holly Langworthy and her baby, he's probably holed up somewhere safe until the blizzard lets up."

"Right." Barring the weather though, she had a bad feeling something had gone wrong. "Let me know if you find anything."

She clicked off the radio and paced across the office, avoiding Lawson's concerned look. All the "ifs" hacked away at her calm—*if* Night had found the baby and woman, *if* he had escaped, *if* Grace hadn't already killed them both.

And what if Grace was planning another germ test? He might already have plans underway....

The phone trilled and Lawson answered it, his expression grave as he cleared his throat. "Langworthy's on line two."

Colleen strode toward the desk. What the hell was she going to tell him?

HOLLY WAS DREAMING again. Someone had kidnapped her baby. Where was he?

Her father…why did she always keep coming back to her father? Did he know something?

"Marry Carlton, it's the best thing for you and your illegitimate son."

"But I don't love him. I can't…"

"Love has nothing to do with this, Holly. Stop acting like a child and take some responsibility. Think about someone besides yourself for once. Joshua. Your mother—"

"But Mother understands. She married you out of love."

"And because she was carrying you," her father said.

Holly felt the words like a knife to her chest.

"Your mother and I do love each other," he said, as if he'd realized his words had been too harsh. "But we were also suited for one another. Just like you and Carlton. He's an up and coming political figure, you can help—"

"I don't care about politics. I don't love him."

Then Carlton had walked into the study. Angry. A smirk on his face. He'd been listening at the door. "You still owe me, Langworthy. I did everything you said. Just because she refuses to close the deal doesn't mean you don't have to hold up your end of the bargain."

Holly sank against the bar. "What bargain?"

"Shut up," Langworthy had said.

But Carlton had known he was about to lose out, and he had talked.

Holly closed her hands over her ears to drown out his ugly words. No...her father wouldn't do such a thing.

NIGHT LISTENED to Holly's mumblings, unable to understand her words. She'd been incoherent for the better part of the day, her fever soaring to its highest. He continued the cold compresses, sought help from the gods with prayers and another ritual around the fire.

"I don't love him," she whispered. "Can't marry him."

He froze again, the pain of her confession hitting him.

"Carlton, no, no deal..."

What? What was she talking about?

He leaned over her and gently shook her, trying to wake her. She barely opened her eyes, squinting through the darkness.

"What about Carlton?" he whispered. "Tell me, Holly."

"Can't marry him," she whispered hoarsely. "Don't love him..."

His hand stilled.

"Why, Daddy, why? No, you can't make me."

He wiped the cloth across her forehead again, patting away the perspiration beading on her skin. "Tell me Holly, what did your father do?"

"Said you would take my baby to the reservation, I'd never see him again." She began to keen then, a low sobbing that tore at him.

"He told you that?"

Her eyes were wide with fear, and he realized she

was delirious. "Want to see my baby. Why won't you let me have him?"

"Shh, he's sleeping."

"You took him away, like Daddy said."

"No, Holly, Schyler's right here with us. He's asleep." He patted her head with the cloth again. "You're sick. We don't know if you're contagious. I thought it would be better not to expose him."

A frown marred her face as if her mind kept jumping back and forth from past to present. He knew it was the fever and hoped it broke soon. He didn't know what else to do.

He shouldn't take advantage of her condition, but he had to know the truth. "What were you saying about your father and Carlton? What happened between you?"

Her bottom lip quivered as the memory obviously returned. "Daddy…made a deal with Carlton, tried to buy him to m-marry me." She shook her head from side to side vehemently. "But I won't do it. Don't care about their deal. Politics. I just want my baby. I know what they said, the news," she whispered. "They called me unfit, said I took a sedative…" her voice broke. "But I didn't know."

"What do you mean, you didn't know?"

Tears rolled down her cheeks. "About the drug, someone, Antonia must have put it in my tea because I was so upset with Daddy."

He stared at her, remembering the way he'd blamed her, that he'd let himself believe every negative thing the press had printed about her. He'd wanted to make her the villain because she'd hurt him. But he heard the agony in her cries and knew she was speaking the truth now.

She had been a victim, too.

He pulled her into his arms, rocking her back and forth, rubbing her back to soothe her. Schyler started to cry, and her eyes turned panicky.

She grabbed his hand, clinging to him. "Dying, Night. I—"

"You're not going to die, Holly. Don't think that way."

The eyes that had once been laughing overflowed with tears, were filled with the inevitably of what Grace had done to her. "P-promise you'll take care of our baby, promise."

He cupped her face in his hands and looked into her eyes. "Holly, don't talk like that. We're going to get out of this, safe and sound, all three of us."

She gripped him tighter, her nails biting into his shirt as his son's cries escalated. "Promise me, Night."

He dropped his head against her forehead and nodded, uncertain if the moisture on his cheeks stemmed from Holly's tears or his own.

He hadn't come this far to lose her.

TEDDY GRACE ran a hand through his wiry white hair and smiled. He had the power of evil at his very fingertips. And he had made too much progress in his research to let that baby escape. "We have to find Walker and Ms. Langworthy and the baby. They have to be somewhere in the mountains. They couldn't have gone very far in the storm with a child."

Bertram nodded. "I've been checking the weather conditions hourly. As soon as we can take off, I'll let you know."

"I want Walker alive," Grace said. "I've discovered some interesting genetic elements in his blood that might be useful."

One day the world would know that he was a genius. Creating a virus like the one he'd used in Silver Rapids, a retrovirus that didn't affect adults, but one that the unborn child had been susceptible to. Just wait until he announced his findings. The retrovirus had enhanced the baby's immune system and could be used as a cure against disease. Excitement surged through him at the ramifications. One day, he might find a cure for HIV. And if this discovery with Walker's blood proved to be as he suspected…the possibilities would be endless.

He would be famous worldwide, a hero.

The fact that he'd been forced to sell deadly germs to Helio DeMarco to support his research was inconsequential. Even if Helio died, he'd find a new source of income. The government could blame themselves for his transgressions. But he wasn't worried. He was already making contacts, searching for the highest bidder…

It just proved how stupid the government was to let him go. Oh, they had professed to be noble, deciding to follow the peace treaties. But they were fools, leaving the U.S. citizens unguarded. They knew their enemies were not trustworthy, that they were preparing germ and chemical warfare to use against the United States. Some already had enough power to wipe out the States altogether.

They should have listened to *him*.

One day they would regret their mistake. All the political do-gooders would be sorry they had fired Theodore Grace.

Yes, they would beg him to come back and save the world.

And only then would he reveal his secrets, let him know just how wide-reaching his germ testing actually extended.

Chapter Nine

Holly's fever finally broke sometime during the night. Night felt her relax into his arms, her constant shivering slowly abating. He sent thanks to the heavens, but lay and watched her sleep, unable to rest himself for worrying she might have a relapse.

Her earlier pleas still haunted him, resurrecting memories of his childhood years on the reservation. The hard years of not belonging, of poverty, of being teased by the white kids he met in town but not quite fitting with the Cheyenne—the years without his father, then without his mother. A child of both worlds, the white man's and the Cheyenne, yet in some ways, a child of neither.

He didn't want his son to suffer the same fate.

"Night."

He shifted, well aware his body had hardened with hunger during the night while he'd lain beside Holly. Entwined with her, bare skin brushing bare skin, her curves tucked into the hard planes of his body, and not making love to her had been torturous. "Are you feeling better?" he whispered.

Firelight bathed her face in a majestic glow, silhouetting her chestnut hair with honeyed hues of gold.

She nodded. "So thirsty."

A slow smile spread onto his face. "That's a good sign." He eased up to a sitting position, the blanket falling to his waist as he reached for the canteen. When he turned to help her drink, she was staring at his bare chest. She glanced down then and realized she was naked, too. Suddenly self-conscious, she tugged at the blanket, although no amount of cover could hide her features from his memory. Once he had loved every inch of her. Had taken her innocence, and planted his seed inside her, a seed that had created their son.

And now, he had bathed that same tender, beautiful skin, kissed it with his prayers and the medicine of his people, every delicate, delicious inch of skin would forever be imprinted in his brain.

Her hand trembled slightly as she gripped the cup. She drank so greedily, he finally had to take the canteen. "Not too fast. Are you hungry?"

Her gaze locked with his, a heartbeat of silence stretching between them.

"I can make some broth if you think you can hold it down."

"Maybe in a bit." She relaxed, lying back onto the pillow he'd formed with her shirt and stared up at him. "Your face?"

He touched the paint beneath his eyes. "To go with the ritual prayers."

She nodded, seemingly accepting his odd answer. "How long have we been here?"

"Two days."

She glanced across the interior of the cave, searching. When she spotted Schyler snuggled beneath the other blanket asleep, she smiled.

"I tried to put him on his back, but he rolls over and sleeps with his rump stuck in the air," Night said quietly.

"You've been taking care of both of us."

He reached out and tucked a strand of her tangled hair behind her ear. "Of course."

"I'm sorry I've been so much trouble."

He lifted her chin with the pad of his thumb, remembering the things she'd revealed the evening before. "Don't apologize, Holly. None of this was your fault."

A wary look darkened her eyes as she lowered her head and looked down at his hands. "But you…hate me?"

He closed his eyes and exhaled. "I don't hate you. I never did."

"You were angry."

"There's much between us," he said, knowing it was true. "And much to discuss when we return to Denver. But for now, you must focus on recovering your energy so we can travel again."

A frown creased her brow as if she was suddenly remembering the night before. "We talked last night?"

"Yes."

She hesitated, sadness robbing those pretty green eyes of the life he'd seen in them moments earlier. "I told you about Carlton?"

Her gaze locked with his again, the pain and grief so strong he couldn't resist. He nodded, then low-

ered his mouth and kissed her, determined to ease
her anguish, even if it was just for a little while.

HOLLY TOOK solace in Night's arms, trying to ban-
ish the humiliating memory of her father's betrayal
and Carlton's sneer that he hadn't wanted to marry
her in the first place. He certainly hadn't wanted a
Native American baby, either.

She hadn't told Night that, had she?

Thoughts of Carlton screeched to a halt as Night
parted her lips with his tongue and delved inside.
She had forgotten how sensuous a kiss could be,
how Night could evoke such need in her by sipping
at her lips. How the sight of his sleek bronzed chest
could make her swoon into his arms and forget reason.

How much she had missed him all these months
and how much she had wanted him to be beside her
when their baby was born. The blanket fell away
from her shoulders as she tunneled her fingers hun-
grily through the silky strands of his black hair. His
hands skated down over her bare shoulders, stroking, strumming her desire, and she leaned into him,
sensations rippling through her at the feel of her
nipples brushing his smooth slick skin.

He trailed kisses down her jaw, licking at her
skin, then lower, but a soft cry broke through the
haze of the moment and dragged them both back to
reality.

Schyler was stirring, had rolled over and was
kicking his feet in the air.

Night slowly pulled away, dropped his head forward against hers with a grin. "He's an early-morning riser."

"Like his father," Holly whispered, raking her nails across the stubble of his beard.

He nodded, then kissed her once again, this time so tenderly that tears pricked the backs of her eyelids. An emotion akin to possessiveness flickered in his gaze as he stared up at her, but wariness lingered there, as well as questions. Then he handed her her shirt and rose. Unashamed of his nakedness, he strode to the rocks where he'd left his jeans, firelight flickering off the corded muscles of his chest and stomach. As if he knew she was watching, his dark gaze latched onto hers, and his sex surged even bolder.

She could almost see him wearing the loincloth of his Native American ancestors, hiking barefoot out into the wilds with bow and arrow to kill the buffalo and bring home food for his family. Battling the elements and any enemy who might attack to keep them safe. Crawling in their tepee at night, the raw savage within him uncontained as he claimed his woman, his name bead necklace his only clothing.

She licked her dry lips, unable to tear her eyes off his muscular backside and the potency of his sex as he dressed. The kiss he'd left her with only whetted her appetite for more.

NIGHT HEATED chicken broth for Holly from the instant packages he'd brought in his stash of provisions, feeding Schyler his morning cereal while Holly looked on and talked to her son. Their eyes constantly met over the firelight as they sipped coffee and ate, a silent acknowledgment between them that things had changed. Uncertainty still existed, but the tension between them had sharpened. Would the flame between them ever be extinguished?

Not until you have her again.

Yet, when they made love, would one time be enough?

He knew the answer, knew that he should resist, just as he'd known he should have months ago. But the draw was too strong.

And here in this cave, they were all alone. Trapped by the storm. Running for their lives. Here he felt as if nothing could touch them. They were cocooned in their own little world. A world where nothing mattered except that they be together.

"Do you want to try and leave today?" Holly asked.

"No." He checked the mouth of the cave. "You need to get stronger. If your fever doesn't return, we leave at sunrise."

She nodded. "How's the weather?"

"The blizzard has stopped, and the temperature's climbing. All good." So, why did he have this feeling of impending doom weighing on his chest? Because he knew they faced danger from Grace and Bertram?

Or because once they left the sanctity of the cave, the magical spell of their closeness would be lost, maybe forever?

Schyler whimpered and began to fuss. Holly started to go to him, but Night picked him up and patted his back, murmuring words of his people, and the baby instantly quieted.

Holly was watching him. "It looks like the two of you bonded."

Night nodded. "He's a smart boy."

Holly laughed softly. "Tell me about the herbs and compresses you used. How did you know how to mix them? Are you a shaman?"

Night sat down beside her in front of the fire, putting their son between them. The baby patted the pile of rocks he'd gathered as if they were toys, babbling and laughing.

"No. On the reservation—"

"I didn't know you lived on a reservation."

"There is much you don't know about me, Holly."

She cast a solemn look his way. "I want our son to learn about your life. Your customs."

His breath sat squarely in his chest. "I told you about my ancestor, North. He was a horse trainer as I am. His name in Cheyenne, Nomeohtse, also means Going with the Wind."

She folded her hands, rested them on her knees. Firelight danced off her cheeks, highlighting her smile.

"He lived in the 1840s, when white men began to settle the West. He knew the white man was coming and wanted to avoid disaster, so he carried messages for fort owners and the U.S. military and government to keep his people safe."

"He was very brave."

"Yes." Night stared into the fire, remembering the childhood stories he had heard of the Cheyenne.

"When North was almost caught, he fled west across the Continental Divide."

"That's how your family came to this part of Colorado."

"Yes. North Walker married Lily, the white woman who warned him that he had been betrayed." He frowned and moved a pebble Schyler was reaching for. It was too small and he feared his son might choke on it. "When my father married my mother, also a white woman, she had a hard life."

"How so?"

"Her parents disowned her. When my father died, she took me and raised me on the reservation, but it wasn't easy for her. Then she died." The reason he would never ask Holly to go with him there, or take Schyler away from her. But what was the answer? It seemed he was following in his ancestors' footsteps....

"Or you either." She reached out and took his hand, and he squeezed it.

Having said too much already, he rose. "I should gather more wood and food for tonight." He tipped her chin up. "Your color looks better. Are you strong enough to watch Schyler while I venture out for a while?"

Holly nodded. "Yes, we'll be fine."

He gave her a long concerned look. "You must rest when I return." Night bent to ruffle Schyler's dark hair. "Watch out for your mama, my son. I will be back soon."

Schyler gurgled something that almost sounded like "Mama."

"Did you hear that?" Holly said.

Night nodded, moved by the awe in her expression.

She clapped her hands. "Say it again, Schyler, say Mama."

"Mama." Schyler squealed with glee. "Mama. Mama."

Holly laughed. Night stalked outside before he relented and touched her again and made himself believe that the three of them could be the perfect happy family. The one he'd never had.

It was easy to fall into that fantasy here in this cave, isolated from the world. But when they returned?

The cold bitter wind whipped through him as he hiked into the woods. Maybe the frigid temperature would bring his head back down to earth where it belonged, and temper the heat building in his loins.

THE TIME without Night should have given Holly a chance to rethink her impulsive reaction to him earlier, but his stories of growing up had only heightened her interest in the enigmatic man. She had always been drawn to his intensity. She saw the same fierceness in the love that shone in his eyes when he looked at Schyler.

But, other than hunger, how did he feel about her?

As the hours ticked by and early evening shadows darkened the walls of the cave, she became antsy. Where was Night? Was he all right? Had Grace or Bertram tracked them down, found Night, and killed him?

Panic scraped her nerve endings, and she paced across the close confines of the cave, adding wood to the fire so it wouldn't dwindle out. She had to stay busy. Not let her mind stray and worry. She fed Schyler baby peas and cereal, laughing as he swatted at the spoon and splattered her with the green slime. By the time they'd finished, it looked as if they'd been fingerpainting with the food.

"You are a mess," she said, playfully, wiping his mouth with a damp cloth.

She heated some water for his bath, then stripped his clothes and washed him. He spit bubbles at her and swiped at the cloth, bouncing his legs up and down as she tried to rediaper him. "You're going to be a handful," she said, laughing as he pinched her nose.

When she finished, she placed him on the blanket with a ringtoy she'd found in the diaper bag, then stripped her clothes and bathed herself, faint memories of Night performing the task for her surfacing. What had he thought as he'd run the cloth over her bare skin?

Again her imagination floundered out of control. When would he be back? What if he was hurt or injured? What if he didn't return?

A sudden sound jarred her, and the hair on the back of her neck prickled. It had to be Night returning. She quickly shrugged on her shirt, then turned as the sound broke through the quiet again. This time she froze, lifted Schyler into her arms, and turned toward the doorway, half expecting Grace or Bertram to appear in the entrance to the cave.

Instead, a wolf stood pawing at the floor of the cave, his eyes glowing bright in the light of the fire, his teeth bared as if he had just discovered his dinner.

NIGHT HAD SEEN the wolf weaving through the woods, and had tried to make his way back to the cave before the animal found the lair, but a small avalanche had snatched his feet from under him and sent him down a ravine. It had taken him an hour to dig his way back up the ledge.

Now he stood behind the animal, a good twenty feet, the gun poised, although he didn't want to use it in case Bertram or Grace were close by. "Don't move, Holly," he commanded in a low tone. "Be very, very still."

She looked toward the entrance, her gaze searching the darkness for him.

"He's hunting for food and shelter," Night said in that same soothing low tone. "He'll move on in a minute."

Her eyes widened with fright but she remained still. He padded closer, shifting his weight so as not to make a sound, then summoned his instincts.

You are a horse whisperer. You can speak to the animals.

"I understand your fear, but I am your friend," he said softly to the wolf. "No one here will hurt you."

Holly shot him another panicked look, and he silently willed her to trust him.

"Animals are not wild," he said softly. "They know what men think and when the hunter wants to kill them. They know how and when to run." He knelt in the dirt and slowly stretched out a hand. "I am not the hunter," he said. "We are not here to kill. Simply to rest and then we will move on, and you will have your cave back, all to yourself."

The wolf cocked its head, eyeing him suspiciously, then sniffed the ground.

"We did not know this was your home or we would have chosen another." Night held his hand very still, relying on the techniques he used with the wild horses. "We will leave come daybreak when the woman can travel. You will have your home back, boy. We are not here to hurt you."

He continued to talk softly, his hand outstretched, while Holly clutched their son in a protective embrace. But Schyler didn't seem scared, he had grown amazingly quiet as if he understood the need for silence. His gaze was fastened on his father and the wolf; he seemed mesmerized by Night's voice. Maybe he'd inherited his father's ability and instinctively knew how to commune with the wild.

Finally, the wolf relaxed its aggressive stance, scratched at the floor of the cave, then turned and moved on. Night heard its lone wolf cry as it crested the hill, as if it promised to play guard for the night. But he held no false illusions. They had struck a temporary deal.

He and Holly and their son would keep their word and leave at first light.

"THAT WAS AMAZING," Holly said. "It's almost as if you can speak to the animals."

He shrugged and dropped the wood near the fire,

adding enough for the bitter cold evening that lay ahead, then began to prepare the fish he'd caught in the stream. Holly relaxed by the fire with their son, playing pat-a-cake and peek-a-boo with Schyler as Night prepared the simple meal. They ate in silence, the earlier tension humming through the air between them.

Then Night told Schyler a bedtime story as he had done for the past two evenings, this time a myth of the Seven Arrows. Finally, when the baby fell asleep in the corner, shielded by the makeshift barrier of rocks Night had fashioned so that if Schyler awoke he couldn't roll too near the fire, Night turned to Holly. She was watching him, the intensity in her gaze skating over him, sending ripples of desire coursing through him.

''You were gone a long time,'' she said quietly. ''I was worried.''

''Were you?'' He approached her, his gaze drawn to the top of her shirt where she'd forgotten to rebutton it. Moonlight played off her soft flesh, so tantalizing.

''Yes.'' She rose then, and indicated for him to sit. Then she moved toward him, and began to remove his shirt.

''Holly?'' He caught her hand.

''You've been taking care of me,'' she whispered. ''Now, it's my turn. You must be exhausted.''

His gaze locked with hers, the tension between them so thick her breath reverberated in the chilled air between them. Slowly she slid his shirt off his shoulders, squeezed the damp cloth, and slid it over his bare neck, then lower to his chest, bathing him the same way he had done her for the last few days. Her hand stilled at the name bead necklace. "This is beautiful."

"It has special meaning," Night said in an uncharacteristically emotional voice.

She paused and touched each hand-carved stone, then dropped her fingers and trailed them across his stomach. The muscles in his abdomen clenched in response.

This time, when he stood and removed his clothes, she was fully awake. She joined him willingly beneath the blanket, firelight painting her body in sultry tones of gold as he tore off her clothes.

He paused, remembering the son they had created the last time they'd come together. Not that he minded… "We can't, Holly."

She frowned and caressed his jaw with her fingers. "Why not?"

"I don't have protection."

Her gaze darted down to his bare chest. "It's okay," she whispered breathlessly. "It's the wrong time."

He stilled, jealousy snaking through him, one last ugly secret remaining between them. He had to know, one way or the other. He searched her face. "Carlton?" he asked in a hoarse whisper.

She shook her head. "No, never." Her hands framed his face. His gaze fastened to her ripe lips. "There's only been you, Night. Only you."

Her admission fueled the savage desire within him, and he swallowed hard before he dipped his head and plunged his tongue between her lips to taste her sweetness.

Holly belonged to him. If only it could be that way forever....

Chapter Ten

Night told himself to slow down, to take it easy, but his passion raged out of control with the need to claim Holly as his woman one more time. He plunged his tongue inside her mouth, taking, seeking, yearning, raking his hands up and down her shoulders and arms. Then he slid them lower to cup her breasts, weighing each soft plump mound before dipping his head to torture her with his kisses.

She cried out softly and bucked, threading his fingers in his hair as he gently bit and suckled at her nipples, frantic to taste each inch of her. She drew his head up and kissed him again, winding her legs around his, rubbing her bare feet up and down his calves and over his buttocks until he was climbing all over her. Kissing her neck, he pushed her hands above her head and tasted the delicate skin, then moved lower again to lick at the hardened rose-tipped nipples, then lower, trailing a foray of tongue lashes across her belly until she quivered.

She moaned and clawed at his arms, but he was relentless, dragging his mouth and tongue over her stomach, her legs, her inner thighs, her toes, then back to the heart of her. His pulse racing, he spread her legs and sampled her honeyed essence, ignoring her pleas to end the torture, by using slow deliberate strokes meant to tease, then pausing, and starting the torture all over again. Finally, when he felt the first of her resistance fade, felt her clamp her legs around him and bear down, giving in to the sweet release of her pleasure, he drove his tongue inside her, drinking in her erotic taste as she soared to heaven.

She was panting then, but he didn't stop. He turned her over on her belly and stretched above her, tracing his mouth over her back and lower to her hips.

"Night, please," she whispered breathlessly.

"Please, what, Holly?"

"Make love to me."

"I am, my sweetness. I am." He rose above her and teased her with his sex, rubbing his throbbing heat between her legs until she parted eagerly, spreading herself wider and begging him to fill her.

Then and only then, did he allow himself the pleasure of plunging into her. She moved beneath him, clawing to get on her hands and knees, and he lifted her, pulling her hips into his heat, moving in and out with the whole of his being. She cried out, again and again, the ripples of pleasure she released spurning his own desire even more.

Then he turned her onto her back, held her arms above her head, and gazed into her passion-laced face. "Look at me, Holly. I want you to see me come inside you."

She opened her eyes then, those beautiful laughing green eyes that were now hazy with the brink of desire he had given her, and she smiled. He drove his mouth over hers and took her mouth again, riding her like he'd never ridden a woman before, and groaning his own release just as the lone wolf cried out on the mountainside in the distance.

HOLLY CURLED into Night's arms, savoring the peace she found in his embrace, tremors of desire still quaking through her. Barring the firelight, the cave was still dark, but morning loomed only a short time away. Then they would have to leave the safety of the cave.

The haven they had found here together.

Part of her wanted to remain here in their private world where nothing stood between them. Not their families, their jobs or stations in life, not the pain of the past or the danger of the future. Just the simplicity of a man loving his woman and child, protecting them and living off the land as Night's ancestors had done so long ago.

He traced a finger up and down her bare arm. "Tell me about the pregnancy."

She froze, startled by his question. Bittersweet memories assaulted her.

"Were you ill?"

She shook her head, unable to look him in the face.

"Holly?"

She closed her eyes, surprised by the longing in his voice. "I had morning sickness at first, but it didn't last long. Then I had the flu in my seventh month."

His hand went to her stomach.

She pressed her fingers over his. "But mostly it was lonely."

He cocked his head sideways to look at her. "Your family didn't dote on you?"

She averted her gaze. "My mother did, but my father—"

"What?"

"He made me feel ashamed."

His jaw locked tight. "Because you were having my child."

It wasn't a question. "Because Josh's election was coming up and I was going to embarrass the family. And…"

"And what?"

"And because he knew I seduced you. That you would never have taken me to bed if I hadn't flirted with you so outrageously."

She sat up then, hugging the covers to her, staring into the firelight. "It seems all the men I've ever dated only wanted my money or sex."

"Your father thought I fit in one of those categories."

She jerked her head toward him. "Like I said, Daddy blamed me."

He sat up then, captured her face in his hands. "You couldn't have seduced me if I hadn't wanted you so badly. Don't you understand that?" He kissed her gently. "And I didn't want your money."

As if he thought he'd said too much, revealed too much of himself, he turned his back toward her and looked down at his outstretched hands.

Holly rose and walked around to kneel in front of him. "Why did you turn away?"

He shook his head, his long hair brushing bronzed shoulders. "Because it is wrong for me to want you so much. To take you the way I did."

Ahh, the power of his emotions were as strong as his sexual prowess? And he thought that was wrong? Didn't he understand that was what had drawn her to him in the first place? The young men in college were materialistic, immature, selfish. Carlton had been out for himself, ready to sell his soul and body to her in marriage to further his career. But Night exuded rawness, a depth of feeling and the natural order of the world that mystified and intrigued her.

She pulled his hands up then and placed them on her breasts, smiling as he moaned with anticipation. "It isn't wrong to share passion the way we do. To feel strongly or want strongly, to care."

Determined to prove that his intensity didn't frighten her, she dipped her head to kiss his neck, then lower to bite at his nipple the way he had hers. Enjoying the tormented sound he emitted, she reached for his sex. She wanted to love him, to prove that her hunger was equally as strong as his. He caught her hands though and pulled her on top of him, so she straddled his hardened erection.

"It isn't wrong for a young beautiful society woman to let a man take her like this?"

She wet her lips with her tongue, then plunged her hips forward to take in his length. "How can making love be wrong when it feels so perfect?" *When it is making love, not sex.*

Heat flared in his eyes, and he gripped her hips with his hands, lowering his head to suckle at her breasts as she began to grind back and forth. He filled her, ignited a burning heat that spiraled through her in hot molten flames. She dug her fingers in his back as he impaled her over and over, his rhythm growing more urgent and hard, his emotions raging in his eyes.

And once more, before they had to leave their private cocoon, they rode the crest to heaven, this time crying out their ecstasy together just as dawn broke the sky.

BERTRAM KNOCKED on Grace's office door, then let himself inside. "The chopper's ready."

Grace grabbed his jacket. "Good. They can't have gotten very far."

Bertram nodded. "According to the map, there's a series of old mines deep in the mountains near Graveyard Falls. I have a hunch they might be holed up in one of those."

"A perfect hiding spot," Grace said in agreement. "Let's go."

Bertram turned to lead the way. "Mary insists on going, too."

Grace hesitated. Helio DeMarco's cousin wasn't the sharpest tool in the shed, but she loved babies. At one time, she'd been a nurse, which he'd thought might be valuable in caring for the Langworthy baby. Years before, she'd been sued for malpractice—accused of killing cancer patients—but the authorities had no proof. She'd admitted her guilt to Bertram, claiming she had committed the mercy killings to alleviate the patients' suffering. Her good intentions sometimes had bad results for others. Grace had taken her on as a favor to Helio. But he damn well would not let her ruin his life's work.

"All right. But you have to keep her in line."

Bertram nodded. "I've already had a talk with her."

The two of them strode from the laboratory, focused on their mission. Grace hadn't come this far to lose one of his best research subjects. And now that he'd studied Walker's blood and had an entirely new avenue to explore, he was more determined than ever to complete his research. He had to trap Walker and get more blood, maybe even test some of his stem cells.

VINCENT RADIOED Colleen. "We've found the laboratory."

Colleen sighed from the other end of the line as Vincent detailed the coordinates. "I'll have other agents dispatched immediately. Do you have Grace?"

"No. No one appears to be at the lab at the moment."

Colleen hesitated. "What about Night and the Langworthy woman and child?"

"No sign of them so far, although we found a woman's coat and a baby crib. Abby and Frank are searching the facility. Jake and I are in Grace's lab now exploring his research files. Colleen—"

"Yeah?"

"There's a ton of stuff here. So far I've barely scratched the surface of one lab, and there's a half dozen more rooms. We've found petri dishes with some weird growths in them stored behind plastic, quick-freeze dryers, centrifuges, eggs he's incubating and there appears to be an isolated area at the far end of the cave that looks like it might be a decontamination chamber.''

"Damn.''

"It's going to take a while to sort through it all and figure out everything Grace is working on.''

"Maybe when we catch Grace, he can save us some time," Colleen said. "I just hope his absence doesn't mean he's moved locations or skipped the country. I'll inform all necessary agencies to alert the airports.''

"He has a chopper, too. We found a private landing pad, but the helicopter is gone.''

"If Night managed to escape with Holly Langworthy and the baby, Grace may be tracking them down.''

"Exactly my thoughts.''

"Michael and Shawn and I will comb the mountains and look for Grace and Walker. You guys stay there and investigate the lab. We'll confiscate all his computers and files and get some experts on them right away.''

Colleen hung up and phoned Wiley Longbottom, head of the DPS, advising him to alert national security to be on the lookout for Grace in case he decided to leave the country. Then she called in Michael and Shawn to brief them on the plan. It was time to end this thing once and for all. They had to find out how much trouble Grace could cause, or if he had already set the wheels in motion to unleash deadly germs on the public, germs that might endanger the entire safety of the U.S. population.

NIGHT AND HOLLY left the cave just as the first rays of sun glittered off the snowcapped mountain peaks. Once again, Night carried Schyler on his back, with Holly trailing close behind, although Night periodically stopped to make certain Holly's fever hadn't returned and to rehydrate them all. Although he wasn't crossing the terrain as quickly as he wanted, a relapse of Holly's illness would put them in jeopardy of being caught, a chance they couldn't afford to take. He had already heard a helicopter combing the skies in the distance and knew Bertram and Grace were looking for them.

"We'll have to take this path." He gestured toward the north. "The terrain's rougher to hike, but it's more isolated and hidden."

"I'm right behind you."

He nodded, surprised at Holly's tenacity. Then again, he didn't know why it surprised him—she had been tenacious in flirting with him. Tenacious in pursuing the kidnapper on her own. Tenacious in fighting to see her son when Grace had captured her.

Holly Langworthy might have once been a spoiled princess, but she was tough, stubborn and a damn good mother.

And an incredible lover.

He could not think about the intimacy they'd shared and focus on the job. Yet, each time he glanced over his shoulder and caught a glimpse of her chestnut hair or that sultry, almost shy smile she offered him, as if she, too, could not stop thinking of the two of them joined together, his body grew rock hard.

Damn. She had gotten under his skin in more ways than one. This time, even deeper, breeching walls he'd built years ago to protect himself from falling in love.

He was not in love with Holly, he told himself. He was simply protective of her because she had given birth to his son.

He veered toward a thicket of trees, then criss-crossed through the tunnel of hardwoods, the ice-coated branches snapping as the growing temperature melted the top layer. Icicles rained down, mingled with new falling snow. Holly stepped into the footsteps he made in the three-foot carpet of snow, occasionally sliding in the sludge. He came to a narrow ledge and hesitated. One slip and he might lose Holly to the jagged rocks below.

"I can do it," she said quietly.

The helicopter rumbled nearer, dipping lower to case the sky.

"Go on, Night. I'm fine."

He gave her a long look, then nodded. "Take my hand."

She did as he instructed. He turned, his face toward the wall so as not to crush Schyler, plastering himself against the jagged edge, and instructed her to do the same.

"Hug the wall, and don't look down."

She took a deep breath, stepped slowly onto the ledge, pressing her body as far into the wall as possible. He hugged the side of the rocks, creeping along the forty-foot-long ledge to the other side, his breath catching when he heard her foot slip and rocks tumble toward the ravine.

"Oh, God…"

"You're doing great, Holly. Just a few more steps."

She had frozen, her nails biting into the protruding rocks, her eyes wide with panic.

"Don't look down." He lowered his voice the way he did when he whispered to the horses. "Look at me, but stay pressed against the wall."

"I can't move."

"Yes, you can," he said, his voice even lower. "You're a strong woman, Holly. You want to get Schyler out of here. You want to see him safe in his crib at home. Picture that in your mind."

She slowly turned her head sideways and he stared into her eyes. "I do want that."

"I know. And it's going to happen. Believe in your own strength."

She slid one foot a fraction of a degree forward.

"You're going to watch him grow up. Learn to walk. To ride a bike."

She dug her nails into the jagged rocky wall, then slid her foot another fraction of an inch. Another and another as he continued to coach her.

"You're doing great. Just inhale, exhale. Slide your foot one inch. Another. That's right."

More rocks skittered down, the echo of them pinging ·into the canyon below a reminder of the vast distance between the ledge and the ground. Of how close they were to death.

"Yes, Holly. Move as if you belong to the mountain. The wall will not let go of you," he whispered.

"Trust your instincts. Let your mind become one with your body and soul."

He continued to encourage her in that same low, soothing tone until her shoulders relaxed, and her steps became less jerky. Finally, they made it to the other side. Sweat dripped down the back of his neck, and she fell into his arms, trembling and panting for air. But the helicopter zoomed lower, and suddenly shots rang out from above.

He grabbed her hand and began to run, remembering the tale of his ancestors, North and Lily, running the gauntlet. Sometime, if they made it out alive, he'd have to tell Schyler the story.

HOLLY PANTED and ran, slugging through the miles and miles of snow, darting into the trees, dodging black grapevines that hung down like serpents into the woods beyond. The wind blew incessantly, swirling icy crystals around her already freezing feet. The dizzying height of the canyon below and the dense brush ahead loomed large enough to swallow them, suggesting there was no escape.

The helicopter appeared through the trees, its blades swirling lower and lower. Mile after mile, it chased them, then disappeared, then circled back, like a hawk stalking its prey, ready to swoop in for the kill.

"A few more miles and we'll be at the jeep," Night said.

But they'd come to a clearing of sorts, a stretch of white that shone bright with the sun. A cliff fell away to the far right, a steep hill climbed to the left. Shots rang out from the opposite direction, as if the shooter was hiding in the great canyon. Night grabbed Holly and forced her to slide down the hill toward the ravine. Her feet slid out from under her, she fell, and skidded on her butt, flying toward trees and rocks. Night was right behind her, shielding her from the bullets zinging through the air.

She screamed, fighting for control, and Night wrapped his arms around her, taking the worst of the fall, and trying to protect Schyler at the same time. Holly's head swam with the dizzying motion. Dear God. The shots had not come from the helicopter.

If Grace and Bertram were in the chopper, then who the hell was shooting at them from the ground?

Chapter Eleven

"Who's shooting at us?" Holly screamed.

"Hell if I know." Night jerked her to her feet and dragged her across the small clearing, then pitched them directly into another nest of trees that choked the hillside. Gigantic trunks covered in snow lifted their branches toward the heavens where a hawk circled, searching for the dead. Their panting breaths hurled into the air, the sounds of footsteps crunching the hardpacked snow below their feet adding to the tension. The fecund smells of growth and decay whirled stronger here, making the hairs on the back of Night's neck raise. He paused, craning his ears to discern the location of the helicopter and other shooter. The squawk of the metal bird overhead broke the quiet.

"Where are we?" Holly asked, panting.

"Dead Man's Cliffs." A virtual nightmare to climb.

"How do we get out?"

"We go straight through it. If we veer out in the clearing, they'll see us."

Holly nodded, securing her silky hair into a ponytail, the strands damp from exertion. But she didn't complain.

"Let's go," she said. "I don't like this place."

Neither did he. The air reeked of death—the aura of ancient ghosts reminding him of the stories of lost bodies in the wilderness that had never been recovered. Hikers eaten alive by bears or worse, falling into some unknown fate that left the imagination to ponder the eerie possibility of demons. Evils more macabre than human ones that lurked in the misty gray sea of the forest. Legends of fallen soldiers, battles with the Crows, the heinous Sun Dance and the sacrificial rituals that had eventually been banned because they were so barbaric, the ghosts of the dead...

Shaking off the sense of imminent danger, he adjusted Schyler on his back, grateful the boy was a trooper, then tied a rope around his waist and connected it to Holly so he wouldn't lose her. Then he could also pull her along. As he climbed through the tangle of vines and trees, clearing the worst of the overgrown brush with a knife he took from the backpack, he created his own footpath. Branches slapped his face, thorny bushes clawed at his jeans, and a few times the low careening sound of an injured animal gave him pause. Where one was injured, a larger one fed. The order of the universe. A universe Grace thought he had the right to own.

To seek and destroy for his own sick pleasure. And all in the name of progress.

Holly tripped, the sound of her yelp making him stop. He turned and helped her up. "Are you okay?"

"Yes, I just twisted my ankle on one of those vines, but it's not bad."

Again her fortitude and determination impressed him. He squeezed her hand, then they continued. They walked for what seemed like hours, the endless miles of trees and the uphill climb grating on his nerves. The helicopter soared above, scratching a path in the sky that dogged their movements. But they seemed to have temporarily evaded the on-ground shooter. One of Grace's hired guns? If not, who?

Finally, they crossed the Continental Divide. They were getting closer to the jeep's location. He picked up the pace, urging Holly forward. "We're almost there. Then we can radio for help."

Seconds later, footfalls sounded behind him. Damn. He paused. Twigs snapped. Branches broke and birds stirred above. Snow fluttered from the trees. The low click of a gun being cocked cut through the chill.

The shooter had found them.

Night headed to the right, grabbed Holly's hand and began to run. They had to make it to the jeep. He needed to go left, but the helicopter roared, circling above in the distance. Damn it. They'd be open targets if they went that way. But they were cornered on two sides. He turned west, weaving in and out until the swell of trees thinned and opened up. The river raged nearby, crashing over rocks. They could follow it to the jeep.

But when they exited the mouth of the woods, they hit an impasse. A huge cliff overlooked the river. Damn. Boots crunched nearby. The sound of limbs being broken, their attacker closing in on their heels.

The helicopter swooped from beyond the trees, circling lower. Grace and Bertram had spotted them.

There was nowhere to run. Nowhere to hide.

"What do we do now?"

He turned to Holly. Saw the fear in her eyes. His son babbled a small cry.

Was everything going to be lost here on the mountainside? Would Grace get Schyler again? Would the mad scientist kill Night and Holly?

No. He couldn't let that happen.

His heart pounded as she clutched his hand.

He needed help. Help from the spirits of his ancestors. He pulled her beneath a mammoth oak and closed his eyes. A voice whispered inside his head. The voice of North Walker.

Trust what you sense, not what you see.

His gaze shot to the edge of the cliff. To the river below. He remembered their location. The Continental Divide. The story of Lillian's Leap.

When North and Lily had been trapped, they'd jumped off a cliff to a ledge below, then jumped into the river and escaped. Could this be the legendary cliff where they had taken their famous leap?

Could he and Holly survive if they took the leap as well? Even if they made it into the river, the temperature this year could be dangerous. Holly had been sick. Schyler was a baby. Hypothermia was a possibility.

A shot rang through the knot of trees, pinging in their direction. He jerked Holly's head down and covered her with his body. The helicopter lobbed downward, searching for a safe landing place.

The voice spoke to him again. *Trust what you sense, not what you see.*

''What are we going to do?'' Holly cried.

He gathered her in his arms, forced her to look into his eyes. ''I know you can swim, Holly. I used to watch you on the estate.'' Those days had been torturous. He'd desperately wanted to join her in that pool.

She nodded, her wary gaze darting toward the cliff. ''But—''

''We can make it,'' he said in a low soothing tone, the same one he'd used to coach her across the ledge.

She shook her head. ''It must be over seventy feet down to the river.''

He nodded. ''Remember the story I told you about Lillian's Leap?''

She searched his face, biting on her lip. ''But that's a legend, not real.''

''I have to trust my instincts, Holly.'' He stroked her jaw with the back of his hand, beseeching her with his eyes. ''Do you trust me?''

She hesitated so long Night heard the helicopter grinding down. Another shot pinged the treetops, closer this time. He fired back, hoping to scare off the sniper.

''We'll make it,'' he promised. ''I will not let you or our son die.''

She inhaled sharply, snow crystals melting on her russet colored eyelashes as she nodded.

''Stay down low until we reach the edge.''

She did as he instructed, the two of them hunkering along the cliff until he spotted the ledge below. Around thirty feet. They could skid down it. Then another thirty feet or more into the water.

He secured Schyler on his chest. "Hold on tight."

He met her gaze, offered her silent reassurance and a quick kiss, then they both took a deep breath. Together they slid down the ledge. Holly clung to Night while he propelled them toward the ledge, bracing himself to catch her in case she missed it. He landed first, and caught her coming down. Her right foot hit the edge and she flailed for her balance, teetering on the brink.

He clutched her fingers, dragging her onto the narrow stoop. Gasping for air, she collapsed, then crawled to her knees. He gave her a minute to steady her nerves, then helped her stand.

"Night..." She trapped his hand, kissed the baby. "Promise me that if I don't make it, you'll take Sky—"

"You asked me that once before." He kissed her one last time. "We will all make it, Holly. Trust. That's all you need to do. Trust and swim like the devil."

She nodded an okay, took his hand, and closed her eyes. Footsteps pounded the snowpacked ground above, sending rocks and snow clumps raining down off the side. Another shot hit the rocks, this one so close, Night pushed Holly into the wall of the ledge to avoid it, shielding her with his body.

''On the count of three,'' he said in a husky voice. ''One, two, three!''

They soared off the ledge together, falling, falling, falling…

THE FRIGID WATER enveloped Holly, the raging current robbing her of breath as she sank beneath the powerful force. She screamed and flailed her arms, gulping in huge mouthfuls of water as the undercurrent dragged her into its clutches. Her feet felt heavy, and the eddies were so strong, the frigid temperature numbed her lips and skin, seeping to her bones. But Night's words echoed in her head. *Trust. And swim.* He had their baby. Schyler was crying, but at least he was alive.

She wanted to hold them both again.

Forcing her panic away, she focused on not fighting and relaxed her limbs so that she could float, giving in to the current. It swept her downstream. She used her arms and legs to paddle, but the jagged rocks beat her skin, nailed her in the back and side. She bit her lip, and tasted blood. But she'd lost sight of Night. Was Schyler okay?

She squinted through the blinding water, spotted Night's head bobbing up and down with the current a few feet away. Her son's head matched the same rhythm, his cry echoing in the wind. Night was searching for her, too. He paddled toward her, then reached back to grab her.

She crawled forward, letting the force of the water propel her.

''Take my hand,'' Night yelled.

She reached out and missed, the current sucking her sideways.

"There's a clearing down there!" Night yelled over the loud gush of the river. He pointed to an underhang. "Try to swim to the right."

Her arms ached. Exhaustion and the cold suffocated her. But she couldn't give up. The rocks tore at her legs and arms, but she finally managed to swim to the edge. Gasping for air, she latched onto a tangled vine draped from one of the massive trees at the edge of the river. Night had climbed out, was on his knees on the ground, reaching for her. She pulled herself toward the shore, yanking herself along with the vine until she touched his hand. Then he dragged her onto the ground. She spit out water, her legs and feet completely numb. Sky was still crying, flailing his arms and legs.

"Let's get him warm," Holly said. She took the baby and began to rub his arms and legs.

"He's a natural born swimmer." Night helped her warm their son, took dry clothes from the waterproof backpack and redressed him.

"Thank you for saving us," Holly whispered as Sky quieted. Night circled his arms around them both. "I told you to trust," he said softly, "but now we must get going. Grace may still be looking for us."

DAMN IT. He'd lost them!

And just when he'd been so close. So close he could feel the blood on his hands. Taste the delicious revenge hot on his mouth.

He hid in the shadows of the bushes, eyeing the

cliff with trepidation. There was no way they could have survived the jump...no way.

Was there?

And even if they had made it into the river, the temperature would freeze them to death within a few minutes. Not the same as actually pulling the trigger himself, but he pictured Holly's body being washed up, all broken and battered from the rocks, those green eyes staring wide-open in death.

Satisfaction sang through him.

Samuel would be devastated when he saw that picture in the paper. And poor weak Celia, she would take her daughter's death hard.

And Joshua... Well, Joshua loved his family. He would feel responsible. Maybe so guilty and distraught he would be unable to carry out his term of office.

HOLLY FOLLOWED Night, relieved when she spotted the jeep hidden beneath a cluster of branches. The helicopter rumbled again. Bertram and Grace had tracked them along the water, and were descending. He and Holly ran toward the jeep. They'd almost reached it when the helicopter swooped down in the clearing in front of them. The propeller whirled around, the force knocking her down, and scattering snowflakes like a dust storm.

Night yanked Holly behind a cluster of rocks, then shifted so he could peek over the edge. He poised his gun, ready to fire. But just as Bertram opened the door to the chopper, another loud rumbling spun through the air, soaring toward them. Night glanced up and breathed a sigh of relief.

''Who is that?'' Holly whispered.

''Reinforcements.'' Night gave her arm a squeeze. ''Sweetheart, we've just been rescued.''

Bertram fired shots toward Night, covering Grace who charged toward them like the madman he was. Mary vaulted from the chopper, dashing on his tail as if the devil was chasing her.

''I want my baby back! Give him to me!''

But a voice boomed from a bullhorn in the helicopter, ''Freeze, Grace, you're surrounded.''

As if to emphasize the point, a round of gunfire pelted the ground in an arc around Grace. Another round hit the chopper, and Bertram scrambled inside. A shot directly in front of Mary sent her screeching to a halt. Grace and Mary threw up their hands in submission, while Bertram tried to escape, but the Confidential chopper cut him off, then landed, blocking off his escape.

Confidential agents Colleen and Michael Wellesley, Shawn Jameson, and Conrad Burke hit the ground running.

Night turned to Holly. ''Stay here, let me secure Grace and Bertram.''

With relief and trepidation filling his soul, Night handed Schyler to his mother, and went to help make the arrests. Night had to make certain that Grace and his cohorts didn't escape this time. And he needed to tell Colleen about the shooter on the ground. They'd question Grace, see if he had a hired hand.

But once they returned to civilization, what would happen between him and Holly? Would she allow him to remain in her and his son's life?

Chapter Twelve

Night approached Colleen Wellesley and the other agents, his gaze trained on Grace.

Grace looked wild-eyed, his beady eyes skating toward Holly and Schyler. "I'm not through with you, I have to run more tests on your blood—"

"You're not going anywhere except to prison," Night said. "For a very long time."

Colleen smiled. "The government has definite plans for you, Dr. Grace. Your own private little lab. Of course, there will be restrictions."

"I didn't do anything wrong!" Mary tried to shake free. "I took care of the baby. He's mine, you can't lock me away!"

Michael cuffed her hands behind her back, and Mary began to wail like a wild animal. Bertram was the calmest one, his gruff angry exterior channeled into threatening eyes. "Helio DeMarco will take care of us. This isn't the end."

"DeMarco is dead," Night said. "So, you can forget the mob bailing you out."

"Or any chance for freedom you think you might have had," Colleen added. "Not only is kidnapping a federal offense, but you and Grace are being charged with treason.''

Colleen's declaration shut Bertram up, but not Grace. ''You have no idea who you're dealing with,'' he said with a snarl. ''Or the extent of my research.''

Night pushed him toward the chopper. ''We'll figure it all out, Grace. We have a scientific genius of our own. Now what germ did you infect Holly with the second time?''

Grace smiled, an evil look that sent Night's pulse racing. ''I didn't give her a second one.''

Mary struggled to get free again. ''I gave her one, I wanted her to die! But you'll never know what kind, never!''

''The government has some powerful persuasive techniques, Mary,'' Colleen said in a deadly tone. ''I have a feeling you're both going to be talking soon.''

''Who was on the ground shooting at us?'' Night asked Grace.

Grace spat on the snowy ground. ''I'm not answering any questions without an attorney.'' Night growled and Michael shoved him inside, securing him to the seat. A second chopper had landed as backup to transport them. ''Find out who the shooter was,'' Night told Colleen. ''He might still be in the mountains.'' Colleen alerted the team to search the area, then radioed Wiley Longbottom, head of the DPS, to let him know they had captured Grace.

Convinced his fellow Colorado Confidential operatives had Grace and Bertram and Mary in control,

Night strode back to the trees and gathered Holly and Schyler to his side. "Come on, let's go. I'm sure Schyler could use a nice warm bath and bed."

"That makes two of us." Holly rubbed her arms to warm herself.

Night nodded and guided her to the chopper. "When we reach Ouray, we'll catch a flight back to Denver. I'll send someone back for the Jeep."

Holly nodded, cradling Schyler to her as Night guided her to the helicopter.

"It's good to see you both," Colleen Wellesley said to Holly.

Holly extended her hand. "Thank you for all your help."

Colleen lifted a hand and brushed the hair back from the baby's face, a grin tugging at the corners of her mouth. "He's beautiful. I'm sure your family will be relieved to have you both back home."

Holly nodded, but Night's stomach knotted. He wrapped Holly and the baby in a blanket and they settled in for the ride back to Ouray.

"I should let my father know I'm all right," Holly said.

"Colleen will inform him immediately. But you can call him when we reach Ouray."

There they'd get a hotel room for the night. Or two rooms, whatever Holly preferred. He knew what he wanted, but he couldn't be presumptuous.

As the chopper soared above the glistening snow-capped mountain peaks and they left the sanctity of the wilderness, old insecurities and reminders of their differences resurfaced. Did he have a place in Holly's bed at all? Or a place in her life?

AS THE CHOPPER ate up the distance between the San Juan Mountains and Ouray, Holly's nerves began to settle, at least her fear of danger.

But Night seemed distant, as if he was drawing back into himself, into that hard shell of a man who refused to allow anyone inside. Maybe he didn't want the other agents to know he had been involved with her. Maybe he regretted making love to her in the cave.

Maybe he was trying to figure out how to take his son from her without committing to her. After all, he'd never said anything about love. Or about his feelings in general.

And she refused to trap him by using Schyler any more now than she had when she had first learned about her pregnancy.

More questions assailed her as they landed and she saw him talking in hushed tones to another agent. His work appeared to be the most important thing in the world to him, and it took him away to God knew where. She still had to sort out her life, deal with her father and decide if she wanted to run those charities for her parents, be a stay-at-home mom or pursue a career.

She glanced down at her son, who'd curled to sleep in her arms, one thumb tucked in his mouth. Those decisions could wait. For now, she simply wanted to spend time with her baby, compensate for all those missed moments the past few months. Maybe she'd take Schyler out to the cabin this spring, show him the warm, beautiful side of the country.

She imagined Night there with them, riding

across the prairie on a mustang, teaching her son the ways of his people, showing him how to communicate with the animals, then in the evening…making love to her until they both fell asleep, sated in each other's arms. Waking up the same way the next morning.

The taxi dropped them at a mountain lodge in Ouray. At first glance, it appeared rustic, but once they stepped inside, Holly decided it had been built to appear that way. The two-story lobby had been constructed of knotty pine, the ambience of days gone by evident in the antique furnishings and cowboy memorabilia along with the collection of Native artifacts framed in brick-red and adobe colored frames.

Night gestured toward the lobby. ''Is this all right or would you rather find a hotel?''

Holly breathed in the sight of the mountain peaks through the plate glass window on the opposite side, where a small restaurant invited guests to relax and dine while they enjoyed the scenery. Nooks and crannies scattered throughout the room housed seating areas surrounding fireplaces, creating a cozy, homey atmosphere.

Not like her home though. The Langworthy mansion was stuffy and formal and required dressy attire. Sometimes she didn't feel comfortable there herself, which was why she often visited the Aspen cabin.

But this place felt as if it had been built with Night in mind. Just like the ranch where he'd told her he lived. Would he show her and Schyler the

Royal Flush? Would Schyler watch him train horses?

"It's perfect, absolutely magnificent."

Night allowed himself a small smile. "I'll book us a flight in the morning. I didn't think you'd want to have to fly home this late."

"No, I can use a few more hours before I face my family."

The silence that stretched between them was fraught with tension.

"Your suite is on the second floor, with a balcony that overlooks the creek." The hotel attendant handed Night a key, his gaze traveling over Holly and the baby. She patted her hair in place self-consciously. He obviously assumed they were married, a young couple with their first child.

If only their life were that simple.

Night led the way. Holly hugged Sky to her and followed behind Night, excitement fluttering in her chest. At least they had tonight together. Maybe a miracle would happen and Night would confess that he loved her.

NIGHT WATCHED as Holly ran a bath and bathed their son, staring in awe at the expert way she handled him. She cooed and laughed, giggling as Schyler slapped at the water, the motoring sounds she made earning a giggle from their son that spoke of pure delight.

She was a natural mother. Youthful and happy and teasing, but careful to test the water before she'd placed him inside, never leaving him a moment while he was in the tub, making certain she wrapped him in the big, fluffy towel in the bathroom to dry him off. Then she lay him on the bed and talked and played with him while Night made a quick trip downstairs to purchase some diapers and a sleeper from the gift shop. They had lost the baby bag in their haste to escape Grace, so he'd also had to phone in for some formula and baby food.

While he was in the gift shop, he remembered that Holly had no clean clothes and neither did he, so he purchased her a pair of warm fleecy pants and a soft pullover, gathered some toiletries, and bought himself a pair of jeans and a sweatshirt as well. He added a pair of black satin panties and a bra to the mixture, his body already aroused just imagining Holly wearing them. The clerk put the sweatshirt on top and he grinned. They would look like tourists with the mountain lodge name emblazoned on the clothing, but who cared?

When he returned, Holly's cheeks were rosy, her eyes vibrant again. Laughing Green Eyes. No matter what happened between them, she would always be his Laughing Green Eyes.

"Can you watch him while I take a bath?" she asked.

"Sure." He tickled the chubby folds of his son's chin, and dressed him while Holly disappeared into the bathroom. Deciding to feed Schyler, too, he busied himself with the baby food. By the time she emerged, baby food covered Sky's pudgy cheeks.

"He keeps spitting it out," Night said, at a loss.

Holly laughed. "That's what babies do. Eating is a game to them."

He glanced up at her, amazed at her self-assurance. Of course, her charm and self-confidence were two things that had attracted him to her in the first place. She exuded sexuality and a joy of life that he had been lacking in his lonely existence.

She smelled like fresh shampoo and soap and the essence of woman he'd tasted before, the one he craved again. His body clenched rock hard just thinking about the fact that she had been naked only moments before. Now she had slipped on the outfit he'd bought, but her hair spiraled around rosy cheeks void of makeup, twirling in long wet waves against her shoulders.

Her gaze caught his, a smile tipping the corners of her luscious mouth as if she realized his thoughts. She had always been a flirt. Now was no different.

She licked her lips, then strode toward him and ran a finger over the soggy baby-food-splattered edge of his shirt. "I'll finish, if you want to shower. Then maybe we can grab some dinner." Holly took a cloth and patted Schyler's face clean.

Night hurried into the bathroom. A cold shower should have relieved some of the ache from his body, but it didn't. Only having Holly again could assuage the constant hum of arousal.

Twenty minutes later, they were seated at a table by the glass window, with Schyler in a high chair smashing crackers on the tray. The landscape looked like a postcard. Through the floor-to-ceiling window, they could see that the gardens behind the inn were filled with bird feeders, which the lodge kept stocked, making dinner a virtual nature show as they watched the winged creatures feast.

Night ordered a bottle of wine and they dined on

steak and bison. Holly had lost weight the past few months, but now their son was safe, her appetite had returned.

"That was delicious." She took a sip of the Merlot and pushed back her empty plate. "I don't know when I've been so hungry."

"It's been a long few days," he said, thinking back. Now that he'd found Holly and Schyler and Grace had been caught, he regretted returning to civilization. But tomorrow he had to follow up with Colleen and see if Grace had identified the other shooter.

"A long few months," Holly clarified. She gazed at their son and ruffled his dark hair. "But this fellow is worth every minute."

"Mama. Mama," Schyler babbled, swatting at the tray.

Holly's eyes teared. "Do you have any idea how much I missed you, little fellow?"

Night's throat closed at the emotion in her voice. He only wished she shared that same love for him and his way of life. But Holly came from money, from fine things. Once her father put the pressure on her again, would she do as Charity had done— choose a man from her own world to spend her time with instead of one with the blood of a Cheyenne?

HEAT ENVELOPED Holly as they polished off the wine and walked back to the suite. Though she was bone tired, she felt very much alive and fortunate to have this reprieve from reality before she was forced to return home.

She didn't intend to waste a minute.

Night carried Schyler to the crib they'd had placed in the sitting area of the suite, and tucked the blanket over him. The poor little guy had fallen asleep in his arms on their way back to the room. Their adventure had obviously worn him out as well. But at least now he was free from that maniac doctor. And Mary.

She shivered at the memory of the nurse's voice proclaiming Sky as her son.

"Are you cold? You're not getting sick again, are you?" Night's worried look moved her. He pressed a hand to her forehead to check for fever. "We can turn up the heat."

"No. I was just thinking about Mary and Dr. Grace."

A low sigh escaped him. "Try to put them out of your mind. You and Schyler are safe."

She nodded.

"Do you want to call your parents?"

She surprised him by shaking her head. "You said Colleen would let them know that Schyler and I are all right?"

"Yes."

"Then I'll see them tomorrow."

He started to lower his hand, but she caught it in hers. "Night...thank you for coming after me and Schyler."

His dark eyes turned black with emotions she couldn't read. For a brief second, he'd let that mask slip, he'd almost let her in. "I don't want your thanks," he finally said in a thick voice.

Her breath hitched. "What do you want?"

He stared at her for so long, she thought he wasn't

going to answer. Then a look of such naked longing filled his eyes that her throat closed. They didn't need words, she decided, seconds later, as she stood on tiptoe to kiss him.

They simply needed to be together.

THEIR LOVEMAKING was intense this time, slow and deliberate and far more sensual than any experience Night had ever shared with a woman. He ordered himself to guard his heart, but as Holly lay naked in his arms, opening herself up to him with wild abandon, it seemed an impossible feat to manage.

She was going to break his heart, far worse than Charity Carmichael had ever done. Because this woman had woven a spell over him with her laughing green eyes, her sassy smile and the passionate way she offered herself to him.

She had also given him a son. A precious gift that meant more to him than life itself.

He closed his eyes as she rode him, imagining the two of them back at the Royal Flush, imagining his son growing up amongst the horse and cowboys, imagining Holly taking his name as he walked down the aisle.

And when she cried out his name in sweet oblivion, he knew that he had lost the battle over guarding his heart.

Walking away from her this time would be damn near impossible.

THE NEXT MORNING, the air felt tense between them as they dressed in silence. Even Schyler seemed to sense the uncertainty between them, and had cried during breakfast.

At the airport, Night checked them in, they went through security, then settled into first class. Thankfully, Schyler took a bottle and fell asleep. Holly wound her hands in a knot. Night had said nothing about the future, nothing about loving her, or wanting them to be a family.

Her parents planned to meet them at the airport. The press would be there, too.

Then everything would change.

HE STOOD in the shadows of the airport, amidst the milieu of strangers and press and Joshua Langworthy's constituents, watching with contempt-filled eyes as the Centennial family walked through the lobby to their private gate, waving and smiling with delight at the outpouring of support and love from their fellow Coloradans. Hundreds had turned out to witness the return of the Langworthy baby and his mother, all having forgotten that the child was the illegitimate heir to the throne of the legendary family. His birth should be considered scandalous. And the man who had stolen the baby was none other than Celia Langworthy's first husband, a crazy SOB who was playing around with germ warfare, a menace to the safety of the American public.

The Langworthys always came out shining like glittering diamonds in the rain while he got nothing.

He itched to exact his revenge in a public way, but getting caught would impede his future plans. He was no fool to justice or the fact that security was at its premium today. Langworthy had secret security teams scattered throughout the airport. They surrounded his home.

He would have to wait.

He knew how to get to Langworthy now. And he knew exactly where to find Holly Langworthy when the time came.

And nothing would stop him. The next time Holly Langworthy's picture appeared in the newspaper, it would be in the obituaries.

Then Joshua Langworthy wouldn't be smiling for the cameras.

Chapter Thirteen

As soon as Holly and Schyler entered the airport, they were swept up in a maelstrom of activity. Her father's private security team surrounded them while he dragged her into his arms.

"Thank God you're alive."

"I'm so happy to see you," her mother whispered through a well of tears.

Holly hugged them both, fitting Schyler between her parents as they each kissed Schyler. He batted at the air between them, squealing as if he knew he was the guest of honor at the welcome party, and he intended to put on a show. Cameras snapped, flashes blinding her, the shouts of virtual strangers yelling and clapping and crying. Her half sister, Marilyn, held back, looking wary and more contrite than Holly had ever seen her. Holly broke the ice by hugging her.

"I'm so sorry, Holly," Marilyn choked out.

"Shh. It's not your fault."

She and Marilyn had had their differences in the past, but her half sister's own pregnancy, now very apparent, had softened her. They had just begun to form a new bond in the past few months.

Joshua crowded in and hugged them both to him. ''Glad to have you and my nephew home, sis. And to have Marilyn here, too.''

''Thank you, Governor,'' Holly said with a smile.

She had never seen her family so close, all huddled together amidst the hundreds of spectators, the gleam of the Langworthy pride evident in the way her father waved at the crowd.

She shied away from the spotlight though, suddenly missing the quiet intimacy of the cave where she and Night had been alone. She searched the group for Night and spotted him standing by the wall, the sea of people between them. He seemed so far away. She wanted to draw him near her, touch him. But she couldn't move for the smothering people reaching out to try and touch her baby's hand. Security pushed the crowd away, planting her firmly in the middle of her father's brigade and herding them toward an exit. She had been suffocated by her father's security all her life. Never allowed to have a normal life. Her life shaped by the family name.

Would it always be this way?

Outside, the questions began. One reporter after another shoved microphones forward and fired questions. ''Were you scared, Ms. Langworthy?''

''Did Dr. Grace hurt the baby?''

''Is it true you were infected with a genetically engineered virus?''

''Why did Dr. Grace take the baby?''

"Did he really want to use the baby as an experiment?"

"How did you get your son away from him and escape alive?"

"Did the father have anything to do with the kidnapping?"

Holly's gaze locked with Night's. She desperately wanted him to take over, to speak for her and their son. He moved toward her as if to answer the questions, sliding through the crowd as soundlessly as he had the forest.

But her father raised a regal hand and motioned for quiet. "The rescue mission was a joint effort between the Department of Public Safety and the FBI, along with private detectives working with Langworthy security. As you can imagine, we're grateful to all the detectives and law enforcement agencies who've worked diligently over the last few months to make this day possible and bring this nightmare to a close." He hugged Holly and planted a kiss on the baby's head for show. "We're just so happy to have them home."

Schyler babbled, swatting at Night's hand, and Night slid a hand to his back, moving up next to Holly.

A blond female reporter zeroed in on the movement and raised her hand. "Are you one of the detectives on the case or is your involvement with Ms. Langworthy personal?"

Night froze and Holly opened her mouth to speak, to announce to the world that Night was Schyler's father, that he had rescued his son, not put him in harm, but Night gave her an odd look and her own father cut her off.

"This is Night Walker, a special detective I enlisted to look for my grandson. He was on the team who rescued my daughter and her child." Her father turned to Night. "Would you make a brief statement about Grace please?"

Night nodded. "Our sources have proven that Dr. Theodore Grace was working on recombinant DNA experiments and making mixtures of germs that could be used either to protect or wipe out large numbers of people. The U.S. government has him in custody now and will monitor his every movement."

"So, he isn't planning a germ warfare attack?"

"The situation is under control," Night said. "The public can rest safely."

Langworthy cleared his throat. "On behalf of the Langworthy family, we owe all of these detectives a huge thank-you." Langworthy pivoted back toward the throng, his comment serving as a dismissal. "Now, my daughter and her son have been through enough of an ordeal for today. My wife and I would like to take them home. Please excuse us."

Holly felt her father and his men tug her along, the security guards imprisoning her in their safety net.

Night fell in behind the crowd, the distance between them widening with every step.

NIGHT HAD HIS ANSWER.

Holly had had the perfect opportunity to introduce him as her child's father and to stand up to

Samuel Langworthy but she had opted to remain silent. To allow the press and spectators to believe he was just another hired hand.

Should he have expected any differently?

The incident with Charity replayed in his head in vivid clarity. Being used by her had hurt back then, but in retrospect, he realized, her betrayal had been trivial compared to the anguish he felt now. He'd been tempted to commandeer the microphone, to set the record straight himself. Only his love for his son and respect for Holly's choice had kept him from doing so.

It was time for him to accept that he would never be more than a temporary lover to Holly. A man it was okay to have sex with in private, but not a man to be seen on her arm in public.

And he would accept those conditions. Even if it meant only seeing his son when she would allow, or when the courts dictated.

Everything depended on Holly.

He hitched a ride with Langworthy's security team and followed the Langworthy limo to the mansion. A flurry of activity awaited them there, more reporters, more of Joshua's followers bobbing welcome home signs to the Langworthy grandbaby outside the gates to the mansion. The crowd cheered when Holly and his son rode through the gates. She waved to everyone as they passed, then again from the porch stoop before being ushered inside by the suits.

"I need to speak with the Langworthys," he told the driver.

"Will you need a ride back to the airport later?"

He chewed the inside of his cheek, then gave a curt nod. He had to check on Grace's research, find out what type of virus or germ Mary had given to Holly. And Colleen still hadn't found out the name of the shooter, although with Grace in custody, he suspected the man had gone into hiding. "I'll let you know what time my flight is."

The driver agreed, and Night slipped from the car, unnoticed as anyone but another of Langworthy's staff.

INSIDE, Marilyn, Josh, the maid Antonia, and Celia all gathered in the living room, gushing over the baby.

"He's grown so much," Celia said. "It's hard to believe he's the same infant you brought home from the hospital."

"I know," Holly said. "He's filled out, and he's almost crawling now."

"He's beautiful." Marilyn looked longingly at Schyler as she rested a hand on her pregnant belly.

"I know you've been through hell, Holly." Josh engulfed her in a brotherly bear hug. "I wish I could have done more."

"You've all been here for me," Holly said. "Your love and support was what I needed most, and you gave me that."

Everyone hugged and cried again, Schyler entertaining them with baby gibberish as they passed him around. "The cook prepared a lovely lunch for everyone," Celia said. "I imagine my grandson is tired from traveling."

"He's a trooper, but he'll probably nap after he

eats.'' Holly scooped him into her arms, and swirled him around. ''Let's go get some food, sweetie.'' Then she wanted to find Night. They needed to talk about the two of them and how they'd make a public announcement that Schyler was his son. He did want that, didn't he?

She'd also been contemplating her future, trying to decide if she wanted to be a full-time mother, help with her father's business, or head the charities her mother worked with. When Night had talked about the reservation where he'd grown up, she'd been moved by the thought of the children there and how they lived. Maybe there was something she could do to improve conditions on the reservations.

Helping his people might prove her love to Night, and she could honor her son's heritage at the same time.

WHEN NIGHT entered Samuel Langworthy's study, the older man glared at him, letting him know without preamble that he wasn't a welcome party to the homecoming.

Even though Night had risked his life to save the Langworthys' grandson.

''Samuel, we need to talk.''

''You think there's a problem with Grace's arrest?''

''No.'' He explained about the other shooter and their speculations. ''But I watched the agents take Grace away myself. I've spoken with Colleen. He's in government custody now. There's no way he'll see the light of day without supervision or be able to get to your family again.''

Holly's father wiped a hand across his forehead, stress lining his face. He had been sweating.

"I expect a full written report on his research," Langworthy said. "And the virus he used to infect my daughter."

"The government and ICU are dissecting his research as we speak," Night explained. "For security reasons, they'll want to keep a tight lid on his experiments. The last thing we want is a public scare." Night rubbed a hand over his neck. "But from now on, Grace will be working for his countrymen, not against us."

Langworthy nodded wearily, then sat down at his desk and poured two scotches. He handed one to Night, then sniffed the other one before he downed the drink in one sip. Night stared at the highball glass, swirling the dark liquid in his hand. He had wasted enough time.

"I intend to talk to Holly about being a part of my son's life."

Langworthy's angry gaze shot upward. "Holly is young and impetuous, but she deserves a chance at a real life, Walker. A life you can't give her."

"I think that's up to Holly to decide."

Langworthy poured himself another drink, this time sipping. "She might fancy she's in love with you, but what will happen once she faces reality? You're constantly in danger." He leaned back in his leather chair and indicated his surroundings. "You can't give her the lifestyle she's accustomed to, and you can't promise you won't die on your next assignment. What kind of way is that for her to live and raise a child?"

Night grimaced. Langworthy had a point.

"And you know how damn hard that child will have it growing up. Teased by the whites, not fitting in with the Cheyenne either." Langworthy produced a magazine filled with pictures depicting life on the reservations. Shots of the poverty, articles about the alcoholism, lack of education…photographs that Night did not need to see in a magazine because he had real memories stamped permanently in his mind.

"Do you want your son to grow up with this as his legacy?" Langworthy cleared his throat. "You know I'm right, Walker. With the Langworthy name behind him, he won't have to worry about being accepted."

The name beads around Night's neck tingled.

He wanted to argue, but the pain of being shunned all his life ran too deep. Barfights. His days of being a bounty hunter. Of not fitting in, of the white man not wanting his hands on their women. Of feeling alone after his parents' death? Of wanting Holly but knowing it was wrong.

With the Langworthy name, his son would not suffer that fate.

He would be educated, enjoy all the advantages the Centennial family could offer, be able to go anywhere and do anything he wanted, with any woman he chose. But if Schyler were torn between two worlds, what would happen to him?

"Here, take this for your troubles." Langworthy placed a folded check in his hand, watching Night assessingly. "You did a fine job of rescuing my daughter. Now, do the right thing, Walker, and let her get on her with her life.''

Night set the drink down with a bang, his chest churning. Anger bolted through him at Langworthy's arrogance. Did he really think Night would accept money in exchange for his fatherly rights?

Still, part of him knew Langworthy was right about some things, that his son would have a more advantaged life with the Centennial family. Besides, Holly had never said she loved him. She hadn't spoken up and claimed him as her baby's father, not in the past seven months or today when she'd been given the opportunity. She probably never would.

And she hadn't bothered to invite him back to the house or to see if he had arrived. She'd treated him just as her father had, like he was simply the hired hand. He'd gotten them home safely, now his job was done. He could fade back into the woodwork.

"I don't want your money." He tossed the check on the desk, and pivoted, moving on autopilot toward the door, his mind racing with uncertainty and the memory of the argument they'd had the night Langworthy had found him with Holly.

Langworthy caught him at the door and shoved the check in his pocket. "Take it as a bonus for bringing my daughter and grandson home safely." Before Night could react, Samuel had ushered him through the foyer to the front door. Night reached in his pocket for the check to throw it back.

But the door closed behind him and he found himself standing on the front stoop before he could even reply. The bitter wind tore at him as did his decision. He loved his son desperately, wanted the best for him.

Would the best be walking away?

His heart hammering, he crushed the check in his fist and dropped it into the flower pot beside the front door, then strode toward the driver still parked out front, and climbed inside the limo. He needed to think. To have some space from Langworthy and from Holly.

"Denver airport," he said.

The name bead necklace felt cold on his chest as he told his son a silent goodbye.

HOLLY STARED in shock as her father shut the door behind him, the realization that she'd just seen Samuel give Night a check slamming into her. Surely, he had paid for Night's detective services. Her father wouldn't try to bribe him to stay out of her life, would he? And Night wouldn't accept....

"Daddy?"

He swung around from the front door, his expression startled. "What is it, honey?"

"Where did Night go?"

He scratched a hand over his face. "I believe he's on his way to the airport."

"Without even saying goodbye?"

He nodded, taking her arm and walking her toward the den. "He came to my office, said he wanted his money, and then left."

"Money for what?"

He hesitated a fraction too long. "Now, Holly, don't worry yourself with these things. You and the baby are back safe and sound, with us, that's all that matters.''

Holly's heart shattered into a million pieces. What about the evening she and Night had made love in the cave? And the night of passion they'd shared at the lodge? He'd held her as if she might break, had been so tender, protective, loving.

And before that, when they'd been running for their lives, when they'd joined hands and he'd told her to trust him seconds before they'd taken the leap off that ledge just as his grandparents had done?

Didn't any of those moments mean anything to Night?

How could he just walk out on his baby after all they'd been through?

She jerked to a stop, and faced her father. ''Daddy, what did you do?''

His eyes glinted with warning. ''Don't speak to me like that, Holly Langworthy. Not after what this family's been through.''

''It was my baby who was missing, my life that has been turned upside down. And I wanted to talk to Night, to try and make it work between us.''

''Holly…'' Samuel fisted his hands on his hips. ''Walker understands that what the two of you had was a fling, sex, nothing more. He doesn't want to be saddled down with a child when his life is in another place.''

Disbelief surged through her. ''He told you that?''

He averted his gaze. ''He agreed that Schyler is better off being raised a Langworthy than a Cheyenne. He can't give the baby the things we can.''

"But, Daddy, I don't care about those material things."

Her father pounded on, relentless. "Did your hero speak up and claim that child when he had the chance? At any time during the past four months? When the reporter specifically asked about the father?"

Holly staggered backward. No, he hadn't. But when he'd first learned he had a son, he claimed he wanted to be a part of his son's life. And although they'd discussed teaching Sky the Cheyenne ways, he'd never spoken of love.

So, what had changed his mind? And how could he have deserted her and their baby without saying good-bye to either of them?

Chapter Fourteen

One week later

Night stared across the light blanket of white covering the six-thousand acres he called home, the Royal Flush. An emptiness gnawed at him that had started the minute he'd left the Langworthy mansion and his family behind. An emptiness that had grown on a daily basis.

Yes, Holly and Schyler were his family.

The name bead necklace tingled.

The first day he'd returned to the ranch, the Colorado Confidential agents had met to tie up loose ends on the investigation. The government had a handle on Grace's research and were making headway in deciphering the various germ concoctions he'd created. Langworthy had reported that Holly had been tested and that there were no residual effects from whatever Mary had given her. Blood tests were pending, but so far the virus appeared to be a flu strain similar to the one that had infected Silver Rapids. They still had no word on the extra shooter, but believed he'd probably gone into hiding.

Things had temporarily settled down at Colorado Confidential headquarters, although there would be more cases to come. More crimes to solve, more horses to tame, one job that bled into another.

None of it seemed to have any meaning anymore.

Because he had lost the only thing that really mattered in his life.

He climbed off the black and white paint he'd spent the morning training and led her to the corral, deciding to reward the horse for her hard work with some free time. She had been so skittish when she'd first arrived that he hadn't been able to go near her. She had made significant strides in the past few months.

Evan, the ranch foreman Dex's nephew, sidled up next to him, hanging over the fence to watch. "Man, I wish I had your knack," Evan said. "That horse was wild as the dickens when you first brought her here. I never thought I'd see the day when she'd eat out of your hand."

"It just takes patience and a good ear," Night said. "Let yourself relax enough to tune in to the animal's fear. Speak to it."

"I've tried," Evan said. "But I just don't get it. I think it's a gift you're born with, just like your heritage."

"You think my heritage is a gift?"

Evan shrugged. "Sure. It makes you special."

Night jerked his head toward Evan. The young man always tagged along after Night when he worked with the horses. The kid was honest, hardworking and thought his uncle Dex a hero.

Just as a son might.

He imagined Schyler growing up here, hanging on to the fence to watch him work, tagging along behind him as Evan did. He saw Holly riding across the field, the three of them picnicking out by the stream. Holly round with another child. Schyler asking a million questions, learning to ride…

How would his own son see him? As a hero for giving him up, for letting him be raised a Langworthy? Or would Schyler resent him, believe Night had deserted him because he hadn't cared? Just as he'd felt his father had deserted him when he'd died… But his father hadn't had a choice. Night did.

And what about Holly?

He'd seen pictures of her in the Denver paper this last week. The Langworthys had staged a big celebratory party to show off her and Sky. The governor and all the powerhouses in Colorado had been in attendance, along with all the society crowd Celia circulated with. Night would never have fit in at the party. His son looked part Cheyenne though, how had he fit in? Had anyone noticed his native heritage yet?

In the pictures, Holly had looked amazing, her chestnut hair flowing over the shoulders of an emerald green evening gown that accentuated those luminous eyes. But she'd also seemed sad. Her green eyes hadn't been laughing. Was she grateful he'd made things easier for her by walking away, or had she wanted to see him half as much as he wanted her?

If she had, why hadn't she spoken up or tried to reach him?

Memories of his mother trying to explain his father's absence nearly choked him. He had blamed her. Would his son blame Holly?

No, but he would hate Night…

Unless he adopted another man as his father.

Night's stomach tightened at the thought, Carlton Sanders's face materializing. Sanders hadn't been in the news pictures though. Night had been surprised but relieved.

Still, something about the photo nagged at him, just like it had the day he'd left the Langworthys after the reunion home. Some detail about Schyler's kidnapping that bothered him early on.

He couldn't quite put his finger on it, but he kept feeling there was something all the agents had missed.

HOLLY ROCKED Schyler in the rocking chair, mesmerized by the way her son grew and changed each day. She should be satisfied with her life now that she had her son back in her arms, but a part of her ached for more. For a while, in that cave, she'd allowed herself to imagine raising Schyler in her own little family.

But Night was gone.

She'd thought each day without him would get easier, but the pain of his loss had spread through her and mounted in intensity each day. Sky seemed to miss him, too, sometimes looking around the room as if he was searching for him.

But Night still hadn't called. Not even to ask about his son.

She'd told herself her father was wrong, that Night really cared for her and Sky, that the passionate way he'd made love to her, the way he'd protected them on the ledge, the story of Lillian's Leap, that it had all meant something. So, why had he deserted them?

Because he didn't want to be tied to her?

"Da-da."

"Yes, I'm thinking about your daddy," Holly whispered. "You miss him, too, don't you, son?"

Memories of the past week taunted her. Once she had enjoyed all the parties at the mansion, her parents' doting attention, the idea of working for her father, handling his investments and serving on her mother's charities, but now...now those things seemed trivial. In the evening, when she lay alone in the dark, she actually imagined herself back in that cave with her son and Night, just the three of them. Safe. Alone. Together.

A real family.

She stood and lay Schyler in his crib for his afternoon nap, then went downstairs to the computer. She'd thought a lot about the Native reservations and had researched their needs. She had an idea she wanted to pitch to her father, but she was determined to present a well-thought-out proposal, one that he couldn't refuse, especially when she planned to implement her idea as a tribute to her son's heritage.

Even if Night didn't intend to acknowledge his son, she would learn as much as she could about the Cheyenne people and pass it on to Schyler.

As she approached her father's office, she heard arguing from the inside. Her parents rarely fought, but Celia's voice rang through the partially opened door.

"You shouldn't have interfered, Samuel. You went too far this time."

"A man has to protect his family."

"Is that what you did? Or are you so afraid of losing your youngest daughter that you offered the man a bribe just to get rid of him?"

Holly pressed a hand to her mouth to stifle a gasp. Her father had made it sound like Night had asked for the money.

"Of course, I was trying to protect Holly. Do you know how many men would pursue her for her money? She's too trusting and innocent."

"I don't believe Night Walker is interested in the Langworthy fortune."

Langworthy's voice rose, "He didn't have to take the check I wrote, but he did."

"No, he didn't," Celia said, furious. "The gardener found your check crumpled up in the flower pot beside the front door." Celia paced across the room. "Good Lord, Samuel, what were you thinking?"

Holly clutched the doorway and pushed her way inside.

"Is that true, Father?"

Samuel turned from the fireplace and stared at her, shaking his head. "I had to see what he really wanted from you, Holly. You've got to understand, Baby, I did it for you."

"You ran him off." Anger hardened Holly's words. "For God's sake, Daddy, he's my baby's father, the only man I've ever loved!" She did love him, she realized, more than she'd ever thought she could love a person. Their first night of passion hadn't been simply sex, or hormones out of control, or rebellious behavior against the restraints of being a Langworthy, she loved everything about Night, with all her heart. Maybe her love would be enough for both of them.

"You may think you love him," her father said, "but he left, didn't he? Without even saying good-bye."

"He must have been upset—"

"Don't make excuses for him, Holly. The man knows Schyler is better off being raised as a Langworthy."

Holly glared at her father, stunned he could be so arrogant. She had to leave. She couldn't stay here any longer. She turned toward the door, but her father caught her arm.

"Please listen, sweetheart. You're hurt now, but you know I'm right. Walker did the noble thing by walking away. It's best for Sky this way, he'll have a better life."

"Noble?" Holly couldn't stomach any more of his controlling attitude. "How can my son have a better life if he grows up thinking his father didn't love him? That his own grandfather is ashamed that he's part Cheyenne?"

Her father blanched. "You're twisting my words—"

"Samuel," Celia warned. "This is between Holly and Night."

"I'm just trying to protect you," her father said.

"You've protected me all my life." Holly jerked

free of her father's arm. "But I don't need you hovering over me anymore. I have to get out of here."

"Are you going to see him?" Celia asked softly.

Holly hesitated. Could she shed her pride and throw herself at Night again? Even though she was furious at her father, he was right—Night had left without saying goodbye. He hadn't declared his love, hadn't even phoned... "I don't know. I'm going to take Schyler to the cabin so I can think for a few days. I can't deal with anything else right now."

She bolted through the door, then headed upstairs to pack. She had to escape her father's suffocating house. Work on her plan. Figure out what she was going to do with her life.

And what she could do about Night.

HE SAT in the dark sedan in the shadows down the street from the Langworthy mansion, biding his time. The pictures of the Langworthy family that were plastered all over the front pages of the newspapers made his skin crawl.

The party should have included him. His face should have been in those photographs, his name in the paper, the people admiring him instead of Joshua.

Joshua, the new governor, the poster boy for the great American family, the Goody Two-shoes who smiled at the camera and kissed his nephew. A Kennedy in the making.

Joshua had robbed him of his position.

And there was Samuel Langworthy, the one who'd pushed his son to run for office.

Then, Holly, the little Miss Innocent of the bunch, the one who'd spread her legs for the detective and spawned the illegitimate baby. The illegitimate baby who had stolen the hearts of the public because of the kidnapping.

It was time. He had just been waiting for his opening. For the moment he could get her alone, without all that damn security.

Holly Langworthy suddenly appeared, driving like a bat out of hell away from the mansion. Excitement pinged through him. This was it.

His patience had finally paid off.

He shifted into gear and coasted along behind, making sure he didn't get too close but keeping her in his sight. Where was she going? To Walker? No, he couldn't let her get that far.

Then she turned. Headed out of town, toward Aspen. It hit him—the Langworthy cabin. The princess liked to hide out there sometimes.

He threw his head back and laughed. Perfect. Where better to end this ordeal than the secluded cabin that belonged to his enemy?

OFF AND ON, all day, Night had sensed trouble. The beads around his neck tingled again for the dozenth time. He couldn't ignore his instincts.

His anxiety had something to do with those pictures and the case. Remembering that shooter was on the run in the mountains, and his concern that Grace had hired help, he once again checked the transcripts of Grace's statement. He'd finally talked, but he'd denied hiring anyone but Bertram and Mary.

Night's heart pounded. That could only mean one thing. Someone besides Grace had wanted them dead.

He had to speak to Holly just to make certain she and his son were safe.

Not wanting to panic her, he reviewed the picture again, then studied the transcripts of all the interviews he and the other Confidential operatives had conducted during the investigation to see if he could figure out who the person might be.

The memory of Holly talking about the night of the kidnapping surfaced. She had been out with Sanders. She was upset with him and her father because they'd made a deal. She'd taken a sedative—no, she'd been *given* a sedative. She'd thought the maid had slipped it to her, but…what if it had been someone else?

When Holly had turned down Sanders's proposal, had he been angry? Would he have helped Grace to seek revenge for her rebuff?

Another possibility—Todd Houghton had not been happy to relinquish his title of governor to Joshua. Would he try to kill Holly to get revenge on the Langworthys?

Night's head was spinning, a bad feeling clawing at his gut. He was just about to call the Langworthy house when his phone rang.

"Hello. Night Walker."

"Agent Walker, this is Celia Langworthy."

Her voice sounded agitated. "What's wrong?"

"Holly left for the cabin a few hours ago. She was upset. I'm worried."

"Was she alone?"

"Yes, I'm afraid so. I tried to talk her into taking a bodyguard, but she's so stubborn."

Damn. What if she was still in danger?

"She was upset, too," Celia continued. "She found out about your conversation with her father. I don't know what to make of everything, Agent Walker. Frankly, I'm not sure if you care about my daughter, or if you simply used her, but she's acting recklessly because of you. Now, what are you going to do about it?"

Night's fingers tightened around the phone. What had Langworthy told Holly about him and their conversation? Had he convinced them all that Night didn't care about his son?

"Agent Walker?"

"I'm on my way to the cabin now," he said. "Don't worry, Mrs. Langworthy, I'll make certain Holly and Schyler are safe."

"And make sure you don't break her heart again, too, will you?"

Night gritted his teeth. "Yes, Ma'am." He hung up, his earlier bad premonition returning.

He hoped his instincts were wrong this time, that Holly and the baby were snuggled in bed sound asleep when he arrived.

But if his instincts were right, they could be in grave danger.

BARRING HOLLY'S roller-coaster emotions, the ride to Aspen had been uneventful. There she had bundled Schyler up with their supplies and decided to take the snowmobile instead of going to the cabin on horseback. It would be faster and safer. She had to consider both now that she had a child.

It wasn't until she neared the cabin that she remembered the last time she had come here and wondered at her own sanity for returning to the place where she had been kidnapped. But Grace and Bertram were in prison and no one else knew her whereabouts. Still, she wished she hadn't left in such a hurry. She hadn't replaced her pistol.

Schyler looked around, eyes wide, from the safety seat, obviously enjoying the ride through the snow-laden Colorado woods. He would love the cabin, too, watching the animals come to feed, the peace and quiet. She drove slowly and carefully to keep her son safe.

Parking the snowmobile in front of the house, she noticed a deer hovering close to the trees at the edge of the cabin. Schyler saw it, too, and yelped. Instead of scaring away the animal though, the doe stopped and cocked its head as if listening. Would Schyler be able to communicate with the animals as Night had?

She carried Schyler in and put him in the playpen her parents had brought to the cabin. He found a rattle and shook it, laughing at the sound.

"Mommy will be right back," she said. "Then I'll get a fire going so it'll get nice and toasty in here."

She brought in the groceries and placed them on the counter, then started the fire. The wood crackled and popped as she fed Schyler rice cereal and fruit. Then she heated a can of soup for herself. After dinner, they played on the braided rug on the floor in front of the fireplace until Schyler yawned and rubbed at his eyes. Then she dragged the playpen to the bedroom, and settled him inside to sleep. He looked around the room and once again, Holly wondered if he was searching for his father.

Once Sky was asleep, she sat in front of the fire, staring into the leaping flames, struggling for answers. How could her father have bribed Night to leave? Why hadn't Night told her? And why had he so readily given up his son when in the beginning, he'd proclaimed his intentions to make him a part of his life?

Did he really believe his little boy was better off without him? Without his father and his heritage?

She wrapped a blanket around her shoulders and stretched out against the pillows, too restless to go to bed but too lethargic to do anything else. Even if Night couldn't love her, she was determined her baby not suffer the trauma of thinking his father abandoned him.

She finally fell asleep on the floor, dreams of making love to Night filling her sleep. Then she was being kidnapped again. Grace…he'd escaped and come back for her. She opened her mouth to scream, but no sound came out. He had another hypodermic, this time he was going to kill her with the virus, and Mary, crazy Mary would take Schyler and raise him….

She jerked awake. A scratching sound at the window sent chills up her spine. Cold air brushed her cheek. She turned toward the bedroom to look for the source. The window was open, the curtain fluttering in the breeze. It had been shut when she'd put Schyler to bed.

The floor creaked. Footsteps echoed on the surface.

Someone was in the cabin.

Chapter Fifteen

Night had flown to Aspen, then rented a snow-mobile and raced toward the cabin, cutting across the less inhabited areas as a shortcut. Although he had never been to the Langworthy's private get-away, he had a map and a rudimentary knowledge of the area and terrain. His mind hummed with questions as he crossed the miles. Before he'd hung up the phone, he had asked Holly's mother who had given her the sedative the night Sky was kidnapped, but no one seemed to know the answer. The maid had denied it. Her parents had been convinced Holly had taken it herself because she was so distraught and had simply forgotten. But Night knew she hadn't.

So, who had put it in her drink? And why?

Someone who wanted her to sleep through the kidnapping?

According to Grace's statements, Bertram had slipped into the house to steal the infant. He claimed to know nothing about a sedative, but he could have been lying.

Since the call, Night had also tried to locate Sanders and Houghton, but neither one could be found.

The runners of the snowmobile shattered the snow, sending icy particles flying. Cold air beat against his face, but he didn't slow down. He had to reach Holly and his son.

He had to know they were all right.

HOLLY FOUGHT panic as she scanned the darkness for some way to protect herself, but the intruder pounced on her before she could reach for the fire poker. She slammed her fist against the man's nose, kicking and struggling, but he punched her in the jaw, and her head snapped back. She tasted blood. But she couldn't give up. If he killed her, what would happen to her son?

"Your family will be sorry for what you've done to me."

Her stomach pitched in disbelief as she recognized the voice. Sweet Jesus, no one would believe her if she survived. He was entrenched in Denver politics, had been a public figure.

"Why are you doing this?" she hissed between dizzying spells.

He yanked her by the hair, his two hundred pounds pinning her to the floor. "Because the Langworthys crossed me. That's reason enough."

She shuddered at the pure venom in his voice and tried to focus on a plan. Maybe if she cajoled him, convinced him she could help him...

"If you want money, we can strike a deal. My father will pay—"

''Yes, your father will pay, but it's too late for money. He has to suffer.''

He wound a fishing line around her wrists. She tried to pull loose, but he snagged the cord so tightly he cut off the circulation. She bucked upwards, aiming for his groin. But he punched her in the jaw again, this time so hard stars swirled in front of her eyes, and she thought her jawbone might have cracked.

''Please,'' Holly begged. ''My baby...''

Tears clogged her voice. She didn't care if she died, but she had to save her son. Even if this maniac didn't kill him, if he left him here alone in the elements, the fire would dwindle, her son would starve to death or freeze.... Dear God, this couldn't be happening. She had been stupid to come here alone.

NIGHT COASTED into the clearing a half mile from the cabin, and cut the engine, listening for sounds. He didn't want to disturb or frighten Holly, yet the voice that had whispered to him on the cliff the day they had taken that leap had returned.

Trust what you sense, not what you see.

His senses warned him something was very wrong. That everything he loved and held dear was in danger.

He parked the snowmobile beneath a cluster of trees, and hiked toward the cabin, listening. Sounds of wild animals rent the night. A lone wolf. An eagle's cry. The sound of fear echoing off the ice-laden branches as they popped and crackled in the night.

Was his son all right?

Slipping through the tunnel of pines bordering the property, he glanced around the perimeter. A single snowmobile. Holly's? Were she and Schyler inside, safe and sound?

A shudder gripped him, the primal fear that had dogged him all day tightening his spine.

Scanning the outer edges of the cabin, he stalked toward it slowly, registering every sound and nuance of animal life. Firelight flickered from the front room, framed in the unshaded window. The front door creaked as it swung back and forth, scraping against the wood floor inside.

Something was definitely wrong.

It was past midnight. Alone in the wilderness, Holly would never leave the door wide open.

One step. Two. He inched up the front porch, weapon drawn, breath hissing into the starless night. The wood flooring squeaked. He paused, biting the inside of his cheek. He was getting sloppy.

Forcing his breathing to slow, he crept inside, his eyes sweeping the room. Empty. His heart pounded as he inched his way to the other room. A dark bedroom, lit by a night-light. An empty bed. His son, asleep in the playpen.

A breath hitched out. Relief. His son was fine. Sleeping peacefully.

But where was his mother?

Then he heard her cry. It pierced the night.

And he took off running to the forest.

HOLLY STRUGGLED against the tree where Carlton Sanders had tied her, the rough edges of the bark scraping her skin until she felt the blood trickling down her arms. She didn't care. She had to get free and save Schyler.

"You won't get away with this," she said, trying to sound sultry. But her voice cracked, sounding vulnerable instead. "Why don't we make a deal? It's not too late."

He circled her in a wide arc, knife blade drawn, gun at his hip. He looked like a primitive animal, vengeance darkening his soulless eyes. She couldn't believe her family had ever trusted this man, that she had. But he had that smooth politician's smile. A smile that did not meet his evil eyes.

He lifted the knife to her cheek, slid the edge down in a caress, dragged it over her chin, across her neck, taunting her. Then he slid it below the top button of her shirt. Popped it off with a flick of his wrist. Then the others, one by one. He snapped them away from the fabric. The brittle sound cut into the charged silence. His foul breath chased across her skin as he ran the knife over her bare neck.

The blade stung. Pricked at her flesh. She felt blood trickle down in a thin stream.

Tendrils of fear wrapped themselves around her vocal cords. Choking her.

"Please, just do whatever you want and get it over with. B-but pro—promise me you'll call someone to get the baby."

His eyes gleamed with the essence of power, the sharp laugh he emitted more painful than the knife blade threatening to pierce her skin.

Then a loud feral sound tore through the air. A wolf attacking? A wild cat in this part of the mountains? Was this his plan, to make her bleed enough to attract the wild animals and let them finish her off?

The sound pierced the air again. A man lunged from the darkness of the forest. Like a black panther, he growled with menace.

Night.

She had never seen him look so powerful. Like a Native warrior from another time.

He dove on top of Carlton and took him down. Bones cracked in the silence. Holly sobbed aloud, rocking back and forth to free herself from her ties. Frantic, she scraped harder and harder against the jagged bark to break the cord, mindless that her blood dripped onto the ground where the two men rolled.

NIGHT LASHED OUT with all the anger and fear he'd kept at bay for the past few months. The sight of this man torturing Holly felt like a brutal blow to his own chest. Sanders screeched with pain as bones shattered. Careening, he rolled to a submissive fetal position and covered his face to protect himself.

The bastard cut a deal to marry Holly. And now he'd tried to kill her.

"You gave Holly that sedative, didn't you? You were working with Grace?"

"I just wanted to be Joshua's right-hand man," Sanders hissed. "Langworthy promised." He spat blood on the ground, his evil glare finding Holly, who hung by the tree, her arms bleeding, her shirt torn. God help him, but he wanted to mutilate this man.

"But you helped with the kidnapping?" he ground out.

"I agreed to marry Holly to get the job as Langworthy's assistant," Sanders said, his words biting. "But I sure as hell didn't plan on playing father to an illegitimate half breed."

Holly's pained gaze met his, tears overflowing her eyes.

"And then she ruined your plans by turning you down, didn't she?" Night asked.

"The spoiled little bitch."

Night landed another blow to his midsection to shut him up.

"You're not good enough to be my son's father," Holly said, her voice cold. "Only one man could fill that role. His real father."

Night's gaze locked with hers, the distance that had seemed so wide between them suddenly closing. He reached inside his jacket pocket, removed a pair of handcuffs and cuffed Sanders to a tree.

Then he stood, wiped the dirt off his hands and went to free Holly.

IT WAS another two hours before the authorities arrived to retrieve Sanders and take him into custody. Meanwhile, Night tended Holly's wounds. Thank God they had only been superficial. Still, she was shaken, and he forced her to lie down.

Finally, the sheriff left with Sanders in tow. The sheriff had taken their statement, then agreed to let them stay in the cabin, so long as they made themselves available for further questioning later.

Night stoked the fire, then removed his coat and

walked to the bedroom. He didn't have a right to touch her, not after the way he'd left things before, not when Holly had been nothing but giving and he had let pride and past hurts get in the way.

But he could not stop himself.

He had to hold her tonight.

He hesitated at the doorway, firelight from the front room casting a golden glow over the bed where she lay. As if she sensed his presence, she stood and came to him. She wore a simple white nightshirt that made her look young and innocent, the virginal princess that he had taken that first night so long ago.

But she wasn't innocent any longer.

And she wasn't the princess he had labeled her to be.

No, she was far more wonderful, more real, more honest, more strong and courageous than he'd ever imagined a woman could be.

"Night…"

"I love you, Holly." The words tumbled from his lips, freeing him, the emotions he'd masked for so long no longer held in protective custody. If she stomped on his heart, he'd survive. But he had to be honest. "God, when I thought he was going to kill you…"

He dropped his head forward, shame and fear pouring out. "I wanted to murder him. To make him pay for hurting you like that."

She clutched his hand. "I'm okay now," she whispered, although fear still tinged her voice. "Schyler's okay. You saved us again."

He raised her hand to his mouth and kissed it.

"I've been miserable without you. I thought that our son would be better off raised as a Langworthy..." His voice choked then, and she lifted a hand, the bloody scarring on her wrists tangling his throat into more knots. "I can't stay away though. I want to be there to protect you, to protect him, if he has trouble being Cheyenne..."

"I don't want you to stay away," she whispered, tears trickling down her cheeks.

"Your father thought Schyler would be better off, and I thought maybe he would be, too."

"How could he be better off without his father? How can I be better off without you in my life?" She wet her lips with her tongue. "I love you, Night. Only you."

She reached for his shirt, unbuttoned it and dropped it to the floor. "I want our son to know you, to know his heritage, to be proud of the Cheyenne ways, to see the wonderful man you are." She rose on her toes and kissed him. "And I want us to raise him together."

How could he ever have thought her manipulative or spoiled? How could he ever have doubted the reason she hadn't stood up to her father? She had been waiting on some sign from him, while he had allowed his pride to guide his actions, pride that had almost cost her and his son their lives.

He stripped the remainder of his clothes, then slowly undressed her, until the only thing that he wore was the name beads that he never removed. And all she wore were the bruises another man had given her. He had to take away the pain and memory of those.

He knelt before her, kissed her hand reverently, then bowed his head and whispered one of the Cheyenne prayers. She squeezed his hand, then knelt in front of him, her breasts swaying, the rosy peaks budding at his loving caress.

"Would you do me the honor of being my bride?"

Holly traced a fingernail over his mouth. "Yes. Under one condition."

"What?" Anything. He'd do anything for her.

"You allow me and our son to take your name."

The name beads tingled, pride mushrooming in his chest. "I would be honored."

Thoughts of his ancestors crowded his mind. The pride of his people. The strength of their spirit. He would pass that on to his son, as Sky would to his own son one day.

Then he took Holly in his arms, and made love to her all through the night, kissing away the pain of the other man's touch forever as the sound of Holly's sweet cry of release broke the early morning sky.

And the lonely, dark emptiness that he had lived with all his life was suddenly filled with light.

Chapter Sixteen

The next day, Holly and Night returned to the Langworthy mansion. This time, Holly intended to tell her father that she and Night were getting married. She didn't care if he approved of her decision or not. It was time she stood up to him and asserted her independence.

"Come on, we're going to talk to Daddy together," Holly said.

Night nodded and gathered Schyler from the car seat, then they made their way into the house. Celia swooped around them, hugging Holly and the baby.

"I can't believe Carlton came after you." Celia's hands trembled as she pressed them against her cheeks. "I never dreamt he'd be so vindictive."

"It was awful," Holly said. "Thanks to Night though, Schyler and I are fine."

Celia turned to Night and extended her hands to him. "I don't know what to say, how to thank you, you've done so much for this family."

"Thanks are not needed, Mrs. Langworthy," Night said in a gruff voice. "I would do anything to protect Holly and our son."

Celia nodded, then enveloped him in a hug, tears overflowing. "Still, you risked your life. If it weren't for you, we might not have our daughter and grandson back at all." Her voice broke and Holly swiped at her own eyes.

Celia traced a finger over the baby's cheek, her adoring grandmotherly gaze tugging at Holly's heart. "Will you take him to the nursery, Mom, and ask Antonia to watch him for a few minutes, then meet us in the study," Holly said. "Night and I have to talk to Dad, and you should be there, too."

"Certainly." Celia cradled the baby in her arms, kissing his fingers. "We're so glad you're back, precious, so glad you and your mommy are safe."

Holly and Night walked to the study, then Holly knocked before they entered, her stomach in a knot. Her father looked pensive, one hand gripping a coffee cup as he stared into the fireplace. He didn't bother to look up when they entered, but remained stiff, angled away from them. The familiar scent of wood polish and her father's scotch permeated the air, reminding Holly of how safe she'd felt here with her father. How many times he'd placed her on his knee and told her stories by the fire.

But she was grown now. She wanted her son's father to share his own stories and life with her baby. And as much as she loved her father, she loved Night as well. She glanced at Night, taking solace in the calm way he held himself in check.

"Father, we need to talk."

Samuel Langworthy nodded, then pivoted, his eyes cloudy with emotions. Celia breezed in the room, moved up beside him and took his arm.

"I owe you both an apology," Holly's father said without preamble. "It seems I made a terrible mistake about Sanders. And...about you, Walker."

Holly's throat closed at the anguish in her father's tone.

"I can't tell you how I felt when I heard...what he almost did to you, Holly." He glanced back at the fire for a moment as if to compose himself. "To think I trusted that man."

"He obviously fooled a lot of people," Night said, surprising Holly. "You had no way of knowing how bitter he was."

"He didn't fool you," Samuel said. "You had him figured out, didn't you?"

Night shrugged. "I sensed something was wrong. I thought that Sanders or Houghton might have been a conspirator in the kidnapping. They both had motives for wanting to hurt you." He cast Holly a smile. "Of course, I had my own reasons for not liking Sanders."

Holly laced her fingers with Night's. "Dad, I know you don't want Night and me to be together, and I haven't forgotten that you tried to bribe him to leave me, but we are getting married. We're going to be a family and raise Schyler together."

Her father arched a brow at them in question. "Is that so?"

"Yes, Sir, it is," Night said. "We would like your blessing—"

"And if I don't give it?"

"Samuel," Celia said.

He threw up a hand to stop her from interfering. Night cleared his throat, his voice steady but forceful. "If not, we'll regret it, but it won't stop us. I love your daughter, Mr. Langworthy, and I love the child we have together. I may not have the power of the Langworthy name to give him, but I will take care of them and love them as the pride of my people have taught me."

Holly's heart burst with affection for her soon-to-be husband. But her stomach quivered when her father's gaze locked with Night's. Then her father strode toward them, and extended his hand.

"You are a fine man, Walker. I was wrong about you, and when I'm wrong, I say it." His gaze remained level. "I apologize for offering you money, but I had to know how you really felt about my baby girl." His cheeks turned ruddy. "You're a father now, I know you understand. A man would do anything to protect his family, especially his child."

A warm feeling filled Holly's chest at Night's forgiving smile.

"Yes, Sir, I do. I suppose if I had been in your shoes, I might have done the same thing." Night clasped his hand and shook it. "Live for the joy of the future, do not dwell on what is past. It is the Cheyenne way."

"It sounds like an adage we should all remember." Holly's father shook Night's hand firmly. "Now, let me be the first to say, welcome to the Centennial family."

Holly thrust her chin into the air. "I'm going to be a Walker now. And so is our son."

"Sky Walker," Celia said, drawing them all into a group hug. "That does have a special ring to it."

They all laughed, the promise of a Christmas wedding almost as exciting as baby Schyler's home-coming.

IN SPITE of the fact that Holly's parents had wanted her to have a big wedding, Holly and Night insisted on getting married in the gardens behind the Lang-worthy mansion. Even though it was cold outside, it seemed fitting to Holly that they take their wedding vows in the place where Night had first made love to her, the place where they had conceived their son. Besides, the light snow drifting down enhanced the Christmas colors, creating a romantic ambience that blended perfectly with the special family gathering.

"You look beautiful, sweetheart." Celia gave Holly a teary hug, then fluffed the tulle of her wedding veil. "I'm proud of you for going after what you want out of life."

Holly squeezed her mother's hand. "I take after you, Mom. After all, we both know you run the show around here, not Daddy."

"Shh, don't let the men hear you. You'll give away my secret." Celia laughed and Holly joined in.

A very pregnant Marilyn, clad in a long burgundy velvet gown, joined them in Holly's room. "Thanks for including me," Marilyn said. "Especially since I'm about to pop."

"How could I have a wedding without my older sister as bridesmaid?" Holly said. "Besides, I want Schyler to be close to his baby cousin."

"I'd like that, too," Marilyn said. "We wasted

too many years not being friends." They hugged, both dabbing at their eyes as they pulled away.

Piano music signaled for them to take their places. Holly kissed her mother, then met her father at the top of the stairs. He looked regal in a dark tux, his smile dazzling. It was too bad his heart problems had cut his political career short. He would have made a great senator.

"Are you ready, Princess?" he asked.

"Yes."

Her father pressed a kiss to her cheek, then held out his arm. "There's something I wanted to talk to you about."

"Now?" He began leading her down the staircase, trailing behind Marilyn.

"Yes. I want to set up a special fund to raise money for the Native reservations in Colorado. I'll focus on education—"

"Have you discussed this with your future husband?" her father whispered.

"Not yet. I wanted to run it by you first. After all, Daddy, look at all the Centennial family did to help make Colorado a state. The way I see it, we're pioneers in leading the state, so why not do something for the Native Americans who first settled our country?"

"Good grief, Holly. You should run for governor."

"Then you agree? Oh, thank you, Daddy. This means so much to me."

He chuckled and shook his head. "I'm serious about a political career. You can be very convincing."

Holly winked. "Maybe I will." Then again, did she really want the spotlight, to always live with security surrounding her?

They'd reached the bottom of the steps, and Holly smiled, her heart fluttering as she spotted the guests through the French doors. Together they strolled through the doors between the rows of red poinsettias flanking the aisle.

Night looked magnificent in his dark suit with his jet black hair brushing his shoulders, his jaw set in a deep smile. Her mother stood holding Schyler and a small white satin pillow which held the rings and a surprise she had for Night. Conrad Burke, Marilyn's fiancé and Night's friend, was a groomsman.

When they reached the gazebo, the preacher asked who was giving her away. Her father said, "Her mother and I," then kissed her cheek and handed her over to Night.

Night took her hand in his, and they stepped beneath sprays of mistletoe and roses that draped the gazebo, their hands wound together as they joined their hearts and souls.

When it came time to exchange the rings, Schyler babbled Mama and Dada, earning a round of quiet laughter from their family and friends seated beneath a white tent in the garden.

"I believe these two young folks have written their own vows."

Holly and Night nodded.

Night took her hand and closed his eyes, murmuring a prayer in the language of the Plains Indians that touched Holly's soul. Then he looked into her eyes. "My people believe that one should not live in the past, but live for the joy of the future. My joy began the day I met you, my Laughing Green Eyes.

"As a boy, I knew only loneliness and darkness, the path between the white man's world and my own an untraveled mystery. But you have shown me the way. You have given me light and love and a son to carry on that legacy. I promise to honor, to cherish, to protect and love you forever more."

Holly bit back tears, then they exchanged simple gold bands they'd bought as a symbol of their union. "You were my protector first, but a night of passion led us to love, then gave us a son. That one evening opened my eyes to the life I had only dreamed of before I met you. You are my Night of passion, my heart, my soul mate. Before I met you, life had no purpose, no meaning, but with you and our son, I have found the light that makes me whole. I promise to honor, to cherish and love you the rest of my life."

The preacher nodded.

"There's one more thing," Holly said.

Night quirked his mouth upward in question, but she simply smiled. This was her surprise.

She gestured for her mother to step forward. Celia winked, and Holly slipped the surprise from the pocket of the pillow—a small necklace made of colorful stones carved into beads.

She held them out to Night. "I had a Cheyenne woman make this for our son," she began. "In the custom of Native tribes, I want him to wear a name bead necklace like his father. The pattern and color of the beads symbolize the Walker name."

Night gripped her fingers, emotions clouding his eyes. "Thank you so much."

Together they placed the beads around their baby's neck, then Night said, "We give our son these beads as a symbol of our love and unity, and to indicate that he has now taken the name of his father and grandfather before him."

Schyler cooed and laughed.

"By the power invested in me, I now pronounce you husband and wife." The preacher closed the Bible. "You may kiss the bride."

Night took her in his arms, and kissed her tenderly. Holly's heart thumped wildly—another night of passion awaited her on her honeymoon night, and another and another...

Epilogue

All of the Colorado Confidential agents and their families had gathered at the Royal Flush for a special Christmas celebration. Since each of them had worked on the Langworthy baby kidnapping in some capacity, Schyler Langworthy Walker was the guest of honor.

"I can't believe this place was once a bordello." Holly traced a finger over the rich, dark pine and red-velvet decor.

"It still has the original old pine bar with bottle racks, the old mirror, brass fittings and cash register," Night explained. He gestured toward the living area. "The living area used to be a stage."

"I love the spiraling staircase," Holly said. "Especially that balcony at the top."

Night chuckled. "The ladies of the night used to wave to their gentlemen callers from there before descending to greet them."

Holly laughed. "I can just imagine the women in their colorful frocks."

Colleen tapped her crystal flute with a spoon to

draw everyone's attention. "I believe it's time for a toast."

Dexter Jones, the ranch foreman, edged up next to Colleen, while Michael and his fiancée, Nicola Carson, joined them. Shawn Jameson and Kelley Stanton smiled from the other side of the bar. Ryan Benton held Helen Gettys to his side, love worn in both their eyes. Governor Joshua Langworthy clasped agent Fiona Clark's hand in his. Conrad Burke and Holly's sister also glowed with love and happiness. Everyone gathered in a semicircle, facing the portrait of Dora Wellesley, Colleen and Michael's ancestress, hanging behind the bar. Wiley Longbottom, the head of the Colorado DPS, assumed the task of refilling everyone's champagne glasses.

Night pointed to another portrait, this one of the infamous and beautiful black-and-white paint horse named Silas, which had belonged to Chance Wellesley, Dora's husband. "That's my favorite portrait in the house. Silas was the reason Colleen decided to breed paint horses," he whispered. "I have him to thank for my job."

Holly kissed her new husband's cheek. "I can't wait to watch you in action."

Colleen cleared her throat. "I'd like to propose a toast to my many times great grandfather and Dora's father, Wild Bill Fitzpatrick, and to Charles and Dora Wellesley for the proud legacy they left us."

"Here, here," Michael said, raising his glass.

They clinked glasses and sipped champagne, the mood jovial. "And I'd like to make one to our new governor, Joshua Langworthy," Dex said.

Marilyn stepped up to his side. "I second that."

A chorus of laughter echoed around the room as everyone joined in with their congratulations.

"And to Con and Marilyn," Wiley Longbottom said. "They're going back to New Orleans to start another branch of the Confidential agency."

"As long as you promise to visit so we can get our kids to play together," Holly said.

Marilyn hugged her. "We're only a flight away."

"One more toast," Colleen said. "To the birth of our mare, Satin's, black-and-white colt. We're naming him Silas for Chance Wellesley's horse."

Night clinked Holly's glass with his and kissed her cheek, drawing her into a private corner. "And to my ancestor, North, who helped us come together."

Holly nodded and added, "And to Miss Lily for trusting in love enough to take the leap."

Night wrapped his arms around her. They had so much to be thankful for this Christmas. "And to our son, Sky Walker."

They both laughed again when they realized the way the two names fit together. Holly kissed Sky's forehead, grateful she'd had the courage to choose a name befitting a Cheyenne's son. Schyler would always be blessed for having Night as a father, as she was blessed by having him as a husband.

*   *   *   *   *

Discover how COLORADO
CONFIDENTIAL *BEGAN!*
Harlequin Historicals
is thrilled to bring you three historicals
about Colorado Confidential's
most prominent families.

Available in January 2004
CHEYENNE WIFE
by Judith Stacy

Available in February 2004
COLORADO COURTSHIP
by Carolyn Davidson

Available in March 2004
ROCKY MOUNTAIN MARRIAGE
by Debra Lee Brown

Please turn the page for an exciting
sneak preview
of CHEYENNE WIFE....

Chapter One

Sante Fe Trail, 1844

"Here comes trouble."

Standing in the shadows of the adobe walls of Bent's Fort, North Walker whispered the words to the horse tethered to the hitching rail. The brown mare rubbed her head against his pale blue shirt, seeming to nod in agreement, but North didn't notice.

The arrival of covered wagons at the fort—even as few as these three—brought news from the East, a chance to trade goods and services, make money.

But this one had brought something else.

Trouble.

North pulled his black hat lower on his forehead as he watched men step out of the trade room, the kitchen, the dining room. They stood in doorways and lingered in the shadows, staring. North's gut tightened a bit, urging him to cross the dirt plaza as well.

Young white women—especially pretty ones—were rare at the fort and in this part of the country. This one, who had just climbed out of one of the wagons, hardly seemed to realize she was the center of attention as she spoke to old man Fredericks.

North kept his distance.

Half-Cheyenne, half-white, North was accepted by the men at the fort for what he was. A horse trader, a guide, a messenger.

His other activities he kept to himself.

Tall and broad-shouldered like his father, North dressed in Western clothing to better blend into the activities at the fort. He had his Cheyenne mother's dark eyes, but his skin was more white than bronze. His only concession to his Indian heritage was his long black hair, tied at his nape with a leather thong.

His father had been a mountain man who'd left his family and a comfortable life behind and come west with the beaver trade; he'd eventually married a Cheyenne woman. North had learned Eastern customs and Indian ways from each of his parents, and was equally comfortable in the two worlds.

Worlds that were on a collision course.

Evidenced by the young white woman who was still talking to Hiram Fredericks, sending four men scurrying to do her bidding.

Stepping out of a hot wagon after weeks on the trail, she somehow looked refreshed and poised. Dark hair artfully piled atop her head, a dress of delicate, light fabric that flowed in the late afternoon breeze. There was an economy of movement as she spoke with Fredericks, a grace North had never seen.

A lady.

That's what his father had called women like this one, North realized. Telling his stories of growing up in the East, he'd described the pampered women there, the hours they spent on grooming, attire and appearance, the value they placed on personal conduct. North had thought it outrageous. Hours spent in the practice of walking? Not to surprise an enemy or spring a trap, but to simply look pretty while in motion?

North had hardly believed him.

Until now.

This one moved like the whisper of the wind, a silent call in the wilderness.

Trouble.

North patted the mare's thick neck, content to keep his distance for now.

This woman was trouble, all right.

But maybe just the sort of trouble he was looking for.

*   *   *   *   *

HARLEQUIN®
INTRIGUE®

has a new lineup of books to keep you on the edge of your seat throughout the winter. So be on the alert for...

BACHELORS AT LARGE

Bold and brash—these men have sworn to serve and protect as officers of the law...and only the most special women can "catch" these good guys!

UNDER HIS PROTECTION
BY AMY J. FETZER
(October 2003)

UNMARKED MAN
BY DARLENE SCALERA
(November 2003)

BOYS IN BLUE
A special 3-in-1 volume with
REBECCA YORK (Ruth Glick writing as Rebecca York),
ANN VOSS PETERSON AND PATRICIA ROSEMOOR
(December 2003)

CONCEALED WEAPON
BY SUSAN PETERSON
(January 2004)

GUARDIAN OF HER HEART
BY LINDA O. JOHNSTON
(February 2004)

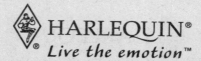

HARLEQUIN®
Live the emotion™

**Visit us at www.eHarlequin.com
and www.tryintrigue.com**

HIBBONTS

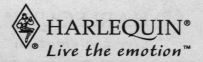

HARLEQUIN *Super*ROMANCE®

Crystal Creek TEXAS

If this is your first visit to the friendly ranching town located in the Texas Hill Country, get ready to meet some unforgettable people. If you've been here before, you'll recognize old friends... and make some new ones.

Home to Texas
by Bethany Campbell
(Harlequin Superromance #1181)
On sale January 2004

Tara Hastings and her young son have moved to Crystal Creek to get a fresh start. Tara is excited about renovating an old ranch, but she needs some help. She hires Grady McKinney, a man with wanderlust in his blood, and she gets more than she bargained for when he befriends her son and steals her heart.

Available wherever Harlequin Superromance books are sold.

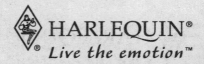
HARLEQUIN®
Live the emotion™

If you enjoyed what you just read,
then we've got an offer you can't resist!

Take 2 bestselling
love stories FREE!

Plus get a FREE surprise gift!

Clip this page and mail it to Harlequin Reader Service

IN U.S.A.
3010 Walden Ave.
P.O. Box 1867
Buffalo, N.Y. 14240-1867

IN CANADA
P.O. Box 609
Fort Erie, Ontario
L2A 5X3

YES! Please send me 2 free Harlequin Intrigue® novels and my free surprise gift. After receiving them, if I don't wish to receive anymore, I can return the shipping statement marked cancel. If I don't cancel, I will receive 6 brand-new novels each month, before they're available in stores! In the U.S.A., bill me at the bargain price of $3.99 plus 25¢ shipping and handling per book and applicable sales tax, if any*. In Canada, bill me at the bargain price of $4.74 plus 25¢ shipping and handling per book and applicable taxes**. That's the complete price and a savings of at least 10% off the cover prices—what a great deal! I understand that accepting the 2 free books and gift places me under no obligation ever to buy any books. I can always return a shipment and cancel at any time. Even if I never buy another book from Harlequin, the 2 free books and gift are mine to keep forever.

182 HDN DU9K
382 HDN DU9L

Name	(PLEASE PRINT)	
Address	Apt.#	
City	State/Prov.	Zip/Postal Code

* Terms and prices subject to change without notice. Sales tax applicable in N.Y.
** Canadian residents will be charged applicable provincial taxes and GST.
   All orders subject to approval. Offer limited to one per household and not valid to
   current Harlequin Intrigue® subscribers.
   ® are registered trademarks of Harlequin Enterprises Limited.

INT03

eHARLEQUIN.com

For **FREE online reading,** visit
www.eHarlequin.com now and enjoy:

Online Reads
Read **Daily** and **Weekly** chapters from
our Internet-exclusive stories by your
favorite authors.

Red-Hot Reads
Turn up the heat with one of our more
sensual online stories!

Interactive Novels
Cast your vote to help decide how these
stories unfold…then stay tuned!

Quick Reads
For shorter romantic reads, try our
collection of Poems, Toasts, & More!

Online Read Library
Miss one of our online reads?
Come here to catch up!

Reading Groups
Discuss, share and rave with other
community members!

For great reading online,
visit www.eHarlequin.com today!

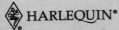
HARLEQUIN®

INTRIGUE®

**Nestled deep in the Cascade Mountains
of Oregon, the close-knit community of
Timber Falls is visited by evil. Could one
of their own be lurking in the shadows...?**

CASCADES CONCEALED

B.J. Daniels

takes you on a journey to the remote Northwest in
a new series of books far removed from the fancy
big city. Here, folks are down-to-earth, but some
have a tendency toward trouble when the rainy
season comes...and it's about to start pouring!

Look for

MOUNTAIN SHERIFF
December 2003

and

DAY OF RECKONING
March 2004

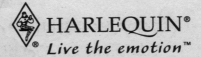

HARLEQUIN®
Live the emotion™

Visit us at www.eHarlequin.com

HICQMS

HARLEQUIN®
INTRIGUE®

Our unique brand of high-caliber romantic suspense just cannot be contained. And to meet our readers' demands, Harlequin Intrigue is expanding its publishing lineup to include **SIX** breathtaking titles every month!

Here's what we have
in store for you:

❏ A trilogy of **Heartskeep** stories
by Dani Sinclair

❏ More great **Bachelors at Large** books
featuring sexy, single cops

❏ Plus outstanding contributions from your
favorite Harlequin Intrigue authors, such as
Amanda Stevens, B.J. Daniels and Gayle Wilson

MORE variety.
MORE pulse-pounding excitement.
MORE of your favorite authors and series.
Every month.

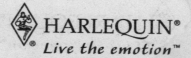

HARLEQUIN®
Live the emotion™

Visit us at www.tryIntrigue.com